Raves for the Wof WADE

"Stunning… like grabbing hold of a line of 110 house current."
> —*Mystery File*

"A pleasure to read."
> —*Edward D. Hoch, MWA Grandmaster*

"Lots of excitement."
> —*San Francisco Chronicle*

"One of the smoothest and most productive collaborations in the history of the genre and certainly the top one in the field of hardboiled fiction."
> —*Encyclopedia Mysteriosa*

"[Miller is] a master plotter."
> —*Chicago Tribune*

"A one-of-a-kind performance, with fascinating detail."
> —*Fort Worth Star-Telegram*

"Tough, lively."
> —*Boston Globe*

"This is hard-boiled noir at its best… highly recommended."
> —*Gary Warren Niebuhr, author of*
>   A Reader's Guide to the Private Eye Novel

Cay got up and, stuffing a cigarette into her ivory holder, stalked into the bathroom. She carried her purse and gun with her. She was standing under the lukewarm shower, gingerly smoking with wet fingers, when she heard the muted sound of voices in argument. She cocked an ear to the wall. The voices sounded stronger near the shower pipes.

She was soaking wet but couldn't spare time to dry or dress. The bath towel solved her problem. When she draped it about her damp shoulders, it enveloped her to the shins. Leaving her shower running, she concealed her purse within the folds of the towel and crept out into the hall.

Another room lay between her quarters and the master bedroom. It was another bedroom like her own, and as deserted. She made a beeline for the bathroom. Next door, Swan's voice mingled with the water of the shower. His wife's voice came more clearly.

"...certain you can't," Concha was saying. "Voluptuous little thing. Be rid of her."

Cay bared her teeth ferociously.

Swan said, "Your jealousy astounds me. When I review your own actions of these recent weeks—"

"Jealousy, no. Sleep with her in town if she represents your taste—but bringing her here endangers us all. I sense she suspects the island."

"I'm certain she does," agreed Swan. "But what's here for her to see? So close your mouth. Besides adding a bit of spice, I believe Señorita Morgan worth probing more deeply."

"Swine, swine without brains! You know she should be killed!"

"I decide what I know, Conchita dear. Hand me the towel, will you?"

Cay drew back from her listening post, seething. She tiptoed hurriedly out of the bathroom.

She stopped short in the center of the bedroom. She was no longer alone...

Branded
WOMAN

by **Wade Miller**

A HARD CASE CRIME NOVEL

A HARD CASE CRIME BOOK
(HCC-011)
July 2005

Published by

Dorchester Publishing Co., Inc.
200 Madison Avenue
New York, NY 10016

in collaboration with Winterfall LLC

ISBN 0-8439-5359-4

The name "Hard Case Crime" and the Hard Case Crime logo
are trademarks of Winterfall LLC. Hard Case Crime Books are
selected and edited by Charles Ardai.

Printed in the United States of America

Visit us on the web at www.HardCaseCrime.com

BRANDED WOMAN

Chapter One

Cay Morgan ceased pretending to sleep as the huge Mexican airliner commenced circling through the tropic night for its landing at Mazatlán. Directly above her forward seat, the warning signs lighted up in two languages, advising her to fasten her safety belt and not to smoke.

A moment later, a handsome black-uniformed steward of the Compañía Mexicana de Aviación appeared from the pilot's compartment and hesitated alongside her, breathing her ever present aura of sandalwood. "If you will please fasten your seat belt," he requested in English. "The flight from Tijuana has been wonderfully smooth, has it not, señora?"

Cay looked up at him through her lashes. "Miss," she corrected him softly. Just past thirty, she grew vainer every year about her ability to make men perspire. She added, with a strange smile, "Perhaps this trip has been rougher than you suppose." The steward continued hurriedly along the aisle of the DC-4 to check on the other passengers.

She knew she was being watched but she didn't turn her head. She reached into her gray suede purse for her compact, briefly touching her tourist card, which told a few details—mostly falsified—about the American woman Miss Catherine Morgan. The tourist card allowed her to visit Mexico for six months, which she considered enough time for her present mission. Before closing her purse, she nudged her gun nearer to the top of the bag.

She had come to Mazatlán to kill a man.

But now, with mirror, brush, and lip rouge, Cay concentrated on painting her soft wide mouth into its usual seductive shape. Only in her most lonely and self-pitying moments did she ever admit she might be merely striking instead of beautiful. Her small but ripely rounded body, sheathed for traveling in a wheat-colored gabardine suit, was constructed daintily in spite of the impudence of certain curves about the hips and bosom. Her flesh everywhere was so smoothly pale and fine of texture that pearls were naturally her favorite jewelry, almost a fetish. So long as her skin was not dimmed by a pearl's luster, Cay could say to herself, Yes, I am still young.

Despite the sultry poise of her figure, men noticed her hair first. It was technically blonde, but silver rather than gold, a hue once called platinum but which Cay herself fondly termed pearl blonde. She wore it flowing to her shoulders so that it framed her piquant face, emphasizing the delicacy of her features. And over her forehead lay a thick straight curtain of pearl-blonde bangs, almost to the arch of her brows. An exotic effect; but the men who'd had the misfortune to know her remembered longest her eyes. They were the sky-blue eyes of a born troublemaker, usually pale with bland innocence yet disquietingly capable of darkening in passion or anger.

She did not look like a woman planning murder; no one seeing her now would suppose that she could hate so long and so hard. She supposed that she could love the same way if she were ever given a worthy opportunity. Always her idol had been money, but she loved herself even more. She had lived through many a reckless enterprise but she had seldom surrendered jurisdiction over her own sleek body. Promises were cheap; she was not.

Having perfected her lips, Cay tilted the compact mirror to survey the plane seats behind her. Then she put the compact away grimly. Both of the men were still watching her. With automatic femininity she pulled her skirt more securely over her knees. Yet she knew the watching had nothing to do with her thighs; it had been too steady and too covert, all the way down the coast from Tijuana.

The big plane made sudden smooth contact with the airstrip and through her window she could see the dark ground race by, slowing gradually. Behind her the passengers stirred with relief and sudden gaiety. Cay began to gather her belongings without once looking over her shoulder.

One of the watchers sat only two rows in back of her. He was the Slavic-looking one, a small willowy young man, not much larger than she. He had yellow hair and his clothing was nondescript save for the fringed scarf of white silk thrown carelessly around his throat. The lids of his narrow slanted eyes hung constantly half closed, sleepily.

The other man sat stiffly upright at the rear of the ship. He appeared more dangerous because there was more of him, a tall gaunt body in a dark pin-stripe suit. He held his hat in his lap, and a circlet of sandy hair fringed his bald head. The lack of expression on his wooden face, his impenetrable eyes like brown agates tokened long experience in waiting. His only movement was his methodical chewing of gum.

Yet Cay was more exhilarated than fearful as the DC-4 taxied to a stop. The passengers, Mexicans and Americans, began their bustle of debarking and she rose to her feet. Keeping her pistol-heavy purse handy, she drew on long flaring gloves and from the baggage rack retrieved the short gray suede coat that matched her tam. With the coat masking the open purse in her left hand, she managed to be the last to leave the plane. The steward gave her a final nervous smile as she descended the steps. She was too busy trying to spot her shadowers to acknowledge it.

The warm night air, heavy and humid, weighed down upon her instantly, as if to prove that she had arrived in the Torrid Zone. It smelled of sea salt and tropical vegetation. She crossed the asphalt, milling with passengers and baggage cars—safety in their numbers—to the airport building. It was a brand-new structure of white stucco and red roof tiles.

The yellow-haired Slav with the white scarf casually smoked a cigarette beneath a palm tree by the field entrance. She passed close to him, neither of them giving the other a glance. She was unable to locate the bald gum-chewing man, which worried her slightly.

No sooner had she entered the one-room air terminal than she was cornered by a plump taxi driver, shirt-sleeved and pressing his stained felt hat to his chest. "You—Mazatlán? Taxi? *Cinco pesos*—five pesos! Mazatlán?"

Her reply in Spanish only confused him until he realized that this blonde American woman spoke the language as fluently as he. Then they conversed more comfortably, Cay requesting that he get her baggage and offering ten pesos to have the taxi all to herself.

The driver plunged away with her luggage checks in his hand. Beyond him, through the window behind the melee at the baggage counter, she saw the slant eyes of the man with the scarf still sleepily watching her.

Cay turned and sauntered through the rest-room door marked *"Damas."* Once within this narrow stone-floored sanctuary she drew a breath of relief. At the far end of the rest room where the washbowls were, two Mexican women were freshening their make-up before the mirror. The large swing-away window beside them stood wide open. Cay pulled it nearly shut for the sake of privacy. Then she closed herself into a booth.

She heard the two Mexican women leave, chattering, as the DC-4 began roaring through its warm-up exercises out on the field. Most of the passengers on Flight 585 would continue inland to Guadalajara or Mexico City. But not the silk-scarved Slav or the tall gum-chewer; Cay felt sure of that.

She took her pistol from her purse and checked it over carefully. It was fully loaded—six bullets—and its chamber spun smoothly, free of lint. It was a lovely nickel-finished pearl-handled weapon with a snub three inches of barrel: a .357 Magnum S&W revolver, the most powerful handgun in the world. At ten paces it could reduce a man's skull to splinters. Cay smiled at the thought.

As she left the booth to go to the washbowls, she sensed something strange, as if disaster waited just outside the door. She piled purse and gloves on the ledge below the mirror and washed her hands, frowning slightly. Then it came to her, the thing she had noticed. The rest-room door she had entered from the air terminal was now bolted on the inside; since she hadn't bolted it, then who...

Other eyes than her own gleamed in the mirror, sleepy slant eyes, a face floating over her shoulder. She saw her own mouth drop open in surprise and horror. She had been stalked by a man into this most private of places, a refuge that her woman's mind had considered absolute.

She didn't scream. She whirled to fight as she was dragged backward, away from her precious gun. But the white silk scarf was already bound around her throat, tightening. Outside, the airplane's engines thundered to a crescendo that threatened to burst her head. She fought wildly with her knees and flailed out judo cuts with her hands and felt her blows land with terrifying weakness.

Then the room got too dim for fighting and she could only claw at the silk garrote at her throat, scrabbling with her fingers for the breath she couldn't find. Above her swam glimpses of the sleepy-eyed face, the open window through which the face had come, and flashes of red and ever deepening darkness. She fell finally into the darkness, which received her gently.

Chapter Two

Saturday, December 1, 7:30 P.M.

She coughed rackingly, then gagged at the impact of new air filling her lungs. The stone floor pressed coldly against her back and her eyes were watering badly. Cautiously through her damp lashes Cay focused up at the face above her.

The face had changed. Now the man was bald, his quizzical forehead and naked skull gleaming in the merciless fluorescent light from the rest room's ceiling. He still chewed his gum, but he was not so woodenly expressionless as he had been on the plane. Cay's eyes dropped to his shoulders, then followed down the dark pin-striped material of his arms. He was squatting beside her prone body. In his left hand he carried his hat; he was flexing the fingers of his right.

Cay whispered, "He took me by surprise, George."

His thin lips quirked with relief but his agate-brown eyes continued to gaze at her worriedly. He said in his flat voice, "You know, I wasn't counting on anything like this."

Cay sat up, made certain her bangs were in order, and wiped her watering eyes. George Hodd simply squatted there, saying nothing more. She said angrily, "If you'll think back to four days ago in Los Angeles, you'll recall that I hired you. You don't get hired by people without troubles."

Not stirring, George Hodd said, "You hired me as an investigator, Miss Morgan. Not as a bodyguard, not as a strong-arm lad. There's a big difference between having trouble and making trouble."

"I'll thank you with a bonus."

"I still don't like it. My business isn't supposed to include violence." He added, "Maybe yours does."

"Oh, don't act so damn fatherly. I'll try to see that it doesn't happen again."

They both got to their feet. He didn't offer to help her. She surveyed the man who still lay on the floor, a bruise swelling the yellow hair behind his right ear, the white silk scarf trailing from his hand like a dead snake. Cay's mouth curled, and in a sudden access of pure viciousness she stooped and cuffed his pale unconscious face with her right hand. The single pearl in the ring on her third finger left a red dent in his cheek. She was glad to see it.

Conscious of Hodd's disapproving eyes, she sauntered to the mirror to see if her throat had been bruised by the scarf. It hadn't. "What did you hit him with, George? You did it nicely."

"I just hit him. You know I don't carry anything." He flexed his fingers again, then put on his hat and rubbed his knuckles slowly. "I think I may have sprained something a little."

She said caustically, "I presume you've been too worried to search him."

She knew better; Hodd was a thorough and competent man, despite his misgivings about her. He said, "Clothes labels from Mexico City. No passport or other papers. Assets, about a thousand pesos. According to the case of his pocket watch, his name's Jack Diki. Know of him?"

"No." Cay transferred the pesos from Diki's wallet to her own purse. She smiled. "That'll help pay your bonus, won't it, George? Did he talk to anyone here?"

"No. On the plane and here, he paid attention to no one but you. When you came in this place, he wandered around to the side. I saw him go through the window. I held off, waiting to hear a disturbance, expecting you would handle him yourself."

Cay laughed softly. "I'm glad you think I'm capable."

"Capable?" Hodd shrugged distastefully. "Maybe dangerous is a better word, Miss Morgan. At any rate, I had to come in after him."

"Jack Diki," mused Cay, staring down at the sleeping baby face. "There must be some use to be made of him. Obviously, he spotted me in Tijuana while I was trying to trace Valdes. Which seems to prove that Valdes is still important."

"But not important enough, you tell me."

"I'm only interested in the man at the top. Valdes is close to the top. Diki here is probably considerably less than Valdes."

"It makes for a bad situation. Now, if you knew the name of this top man—if you even knew what he looks like…"

Cay chuckled. "You want high pay for easy work, don't you? I'm beginning to regret hiring such a timid chap to help me find the Trader. Please snap out of it."

Hodd said patiently, "We'll get along better if you quit mistaking legality for timidity. I've got a license and a reputation to maintain. Furthermore, Diki spotted you. He didn't spot me. Consider that a reference."

"Or a rebuke, eh? But it proves you're elected to do the legwork in Mazatlán. I'm spotted, you're not. It's that simple. I'll go on into town and check into one of the tourist hotels. I believe there are three here. Later on tonight or in the morning, you get a room at the same hotel. But no one must know we're acquainted, much less hunting together."

Hodd glanced down at Diki. "All right. You want me to stick with him for a while?"

"Exactly. You'd better go now. Diki's bound to come around pretty soon and I want you to be sure to find out where he goes. Perhaps directly to Valdes. That would save us a lot of time."

Hodd chewed his gum contemplatively. "You're the boss," he said to Cay finally. "See you." A second later he had folded his gaunt body through the window and was gone. She complimented herself again on picking a good man, all business. She was grateful to Hodd for his quiet negative virtues; he seemed to have no intentions of trying to paw her, of making sly suggestions about the hotel arrangements.

Cay collected her gloves and purse from the shelf below the mirror. She paused over Diki's body. At first sight of him stretched out there, she had felt a little sorry for him, despite everything. His soft smooth face was so childlike and his small frame appeared so helpless, making her wonder what had ever turned such an everyday person into an assassin.

Then she thought of herself. Why was *she* out for blood? And the hate flooded up inside of her as she remembered that Jack Diki was part of the Trader. However far removed, he was part of him; perhaps he was of no more consequence than a fingernail, but nevertheless...

For an instant she was ready to kill the helpless creature on the floor.

Instead she smiled broadly. She murmured, "Perhaps I should give him something to think about." She didn't mean Diki. But it was Diki's smooth forehead that, crouching, she marked with her lipstick. She drew a blood-red letter T. Then she slipped out through the window and walked around the building to her waiting taxi.

Chapter Three

Saturday, December 1, 8:00 P.M.

A cardboard *"Libre"* sign on its windshield was the only indication that the black Pontiac was a taxi. It hurtled along the highway and into the narrow one-way streets of Mazatlán with a gay disregard of property rights. To disguise her fears, Cay stuck a cigarette into her ivory holder and tried to smoke. She had a hard time lighting it. All the car's windows were open to the muggy night air, and she couldn't keep her eyes off the dark faces of the aggressive pedestrians who seemed intent on walking right through the speeding, honking taxi.

"You have a lovely old town," she told him in Spanish.

"Very old, yes. But notice how modern the city, señora. No decaying museum, as some cities pride themselves on being to the *turistas*. Do you come to hunt or to fish?"

"To hunt, I believe."

"Then be so kind as to beware in choosing a guide. The boas and *tigres* can be dangerous—and there are yet bandits in the hills on occasion."

"*Gracias*. I have a modest ability with firearms." She didn't tell him that she had been called a bandit herself on occasion. She got a colorfully blurred impression of the peninsula city, a strolling yet bustling populace in shirt sleeves and cotton dresses. She saw as many Cadillacs as burros, as much glass brick and neon as adobe and iron grillework; flat roofs capping flat façades that rose directly from the high sidewalks, a silver crescent of ocean beach, surf surging toward the sea wall of a broad marble-benched esplanade.

This was the Paseo Olas Altas. The taxi driver parked before the starkly modern tower of the Hotel Freeman, eight of its eleven floors completed, and assisted Cay up to the second story, where the registration office was temporarily located in a guest room. With its commanding height and angular balconies, the Freeman loomed above the city like a great gray filing cabinet with all drawers open.

"I have no reservation, señor," explained Cay with a doleful smile. "But I am alone, and surely one small single room…"

"Please be reassured," said the young man in charge. But he chewed his lip worriedly as he sat down on his stool and searched among the cards on the wooden table. Cay toyed with the postcard rack and looked wistful.

Five minutes later she found herself the lone occupant of Room 22 on the third floor, gazing amusedly around her quarters. Ranged about the clean tiled floor were the usual writing desk and chiffonier, a canvas deck chair, and three beds—two doubles and a single. Very good, she thought, so long as all this sleeping space doesn't give George any bright ideas.

She hung her coat in the closet, pulled off her tam, gloves, and shoes, and explored. Both lock and bolt on the hall door worked efficiently. The bathroom contained a vast shower but no tub, and the transom to the air shaft was too small for even a midget to creep through. Since she had seen bottled water racked in the hall outside, she deemed it safe to drink a glassful from the carafe on the bedstand.

The west end of the room was completely paned in glass, high French doors in the center opening onto a private balcony. Cay lingered out there, leaning on the low pipe-iron railing, letting herself melt into the beauty of the somnolent night. The pungent smell of the city was less obvious here, but the tang of the surf was sharp. A guitar strummed distantly, a man sang. She watched the couples drift along the curving promenade while taxi drivers waited patiently for them to tire. She listened to the faint chatter of shoeshine boys, for this was the tourist quarter, and to the north along the boulevard she could see the Hotel Belmar and the Banco de México and the Americanized *salones de cocteles*. Offshore flickered the lights of some anchored freighter, too large to navigate the harbor channel.

A sentimental lump formed in Cay's throat—until she noticed the friendly arrangement of the hotel balconies. Each concrete platform was inset slightly from its left-hand neighbor, but it would require no feat of daring to traverse completely the front of the hotel by the balcony route. And her balcony was attainable from either side.

The lump in her throat changed to a choking memory of Diki's white silk scarf. She whirled back into her room and closed the French doors, testing the lock. It was small comfort, but she decided any sounds of its being forced would be enough to awaken her. Her blue eyes pale and cold now, she placed her .357 Magnum within reach on the single bed and began to unpack.

Her unpacking was both routine and ritual. Experience had taught her the folly of unpacking any apparel beyond the moment's need. But first of all she brought forth these objects that transformed wherever she was into her home. The table runner of Madeira lace went across the chiffonier. On it she set her brass incense burner and ceremoniously lighted a cone of fragrance. The scent of sandalwood began to fill the hotel room. Its seductive odor already permeated everything she owned; she used no other perfume.

She wound her Swiss traveling clock, set it ahead an hour to Mazatlán time, and placed it on the bedstand. Then back to the chiffonier with two gilt-framed silhouettes, a man's profile and a woman's, which she had bought in a secondhand shop in Rome. Her father and mother, Cay pretended. That was the way she remembered them—as shadow people. Her dead mother had been American; her runaway father, English. Cay's own past was so misted in her own lies and changes of name that she could scarcely remember any true details.

Except for the Trader, five years ago…

Her face had been more angelic then, framed in golden-blonde hair without the bangs. She had been in Morocco, on her own, as always. Her business had involved buying a collection of antique jewelry from a displaced Austrian family and smuggling it to England for sale to an art dealer there.

For such profits there was competition. She was warned against consummating the deal by a skull-faced Spanish pawnbroker claiming to be an agent for the Trader. She had never heard the name before. "Pet," the pawnbroker had crooned unctuously, "I beg of you to let my friend the Trader fence those gimcracks. We have the proper facilities for distributing them quietly—everywhere we have representatives. Please retire from this delicate business like a good girl."

"Why, señor? I'm not a good girl. And you can't do worse than kill me."

"Can't we?" the pawnbroker had replied.

She had been a good enough girl to slip the jewel collection to her outlet in Liverpool without being caught by customs men or competition. But she had answered her door in London one evening to find the Spanish pawnbroker standing there, and a sickly-sweet cloth had been clasped over her mouth and nose, and his oily voice had said, "Easy, pet, the Trader wants to teach you your manners," and she had awakened the next morning in a stinking alley in Lambeth, sobbing with pain.

She had known then that the Trader could do worse to her than kill her, for he had done it.

And she had never seen him, or heard his voice, or known his name. It was a phantom she hated, yet she determined to kill him for what he had inflicted on her. But as she made her way in the world, she learned how ghostly his elusiveness could be. The results of his illicit barter appeared everywhere, but the creature himself remained unknown or unrecognizable to his markets, even to his own dealers and appraisers and agents. She might have seen him many times without realizing it. Every rumor she tracked down had ended in grinding frustration.

Until last week...

Cay discovered she was sitting tensely on the foot of the single bed, one hand pressed flat over her revolver, lost in heated reverie. She stood up angrily and got the brandy flask from her suitcase and poured a drink into one of the pair of crystal goblets she always carried with her. She sipped it, then drew the draperies across the glass-paned west end of the room and stripped off her clothes. She padded into the bathroom, bound up her mane of pale blonde hair, and took a relaxing shower. She wondered where Diki the strangler had gone, and if Hodd could follow him. She was counting a great deal on Diki's providing her with a further trail; the slant-eyed youth had proved to be a lucky break. She didn't expect Hodd to report in very soon, probably not before morning. Then she thought about what a pretty town Mazatlán seemed to be, its quaint crooked streets and warm-lit windows and arm-linked couples on that romantic esplanade. Suddenly, toweling her lovely body, she burst into tears.

She was lonely and sorry for herself.

She pampered her dejection, sniffling occasionally as she combed out her hair and finished her glass of brandy.

Replacing the brandy flask in her suitcase, she came across the ragged newspaper photograph that had brought her to Mexico. Although she knew it by heart, she studied it afresh through her lorgnette, a dainty silver device with a single pearl set in the handle. Lately she had needed an aid for close work, but she would rather be beheaded than wear spectacles. The lorgnette suited her taste perfectly; when it was necessary to use her lenses publicly, she could pass them off as an affectation instead of a weakness.

She had been sunning herself by a swimming pool in Palm Springs, as alert for prey as an animal at a water hole, when she had first discovered the picture in the Examiner. It showed some box seats at last Sunday's bullfights in Tijuana, four Los Angeles socialites smiling in the foreground.

But Cay's eyes had narrowed at an unidentified man in the second row who had not realized a news photo was being taken. He was intent on the action below in the bull ring, his small movie camera masking his right eye and cheek. Yet the visible half of the tight-skinned skull-like face was unmistakably that of the Spanish pawnbroker.

Cay had immediately abandoned all her other schemes. After hiring a muscular assistant in Los Angeles, she had flown to Tijuana, where she learned that the Spaniard had stayed one night before proceeding to Mazatlán. He was now using the name Eduardo Valdes.

Five days behind him—she hadn't been so near in five years. If Valdes had remained in Mazatlán, then something in this city greatly interested the Trader. Indeed, wherever Valdes was, there the Trader himself was likely to be. Older and colder trails had taught her that much. The Trader in Mazatlán... Her hands clenched in vicious prayer, crumpling the newspaper clipping. At this moment he might be taking a nightly stroll on the boulevard outside; he might be as close to her as the room overhead and she wouldn't know. He might be any name on a hotel register, any face in a passing taxi, any nationality.

Valdes knows him, Cay told herself for the millionth time. Valdes can be made to take me to him, somehow. She smoothed the clipping and put it away.

She was standing before the chiffonier mirror and she turned to confront her naked image. She looked at her small waist, her full breasts, her smooth throat. Finally she looked at her unsmiling face. So beautiful, Cay thought. I would have been so beautiful.

Suddenly she raised her hand and pushed up her long pearl-blonde bangs, disclosing the high sweep of her brow. Abruptly she was ugly. She stood staring, breath held, torturing herself anew with what had been branded on her forehead.

Five years had smoothed the scar's puckered edges,

but the deep brand of the T was still gullied in her skin like a pale headless crucifix.

Chapter Four

Saturday, December 1, 9:00 P.M.

"Well, I'm registered in the room right over your head," said Hodd, sinking down into the canvas deck chair. "I think we share the same air shaft." He mopped his bald head and gave a dejected chuckle. "I think I've been slighted—my room only sleeps four."

"What are you doing here so soon?" Cay asked between her teeth. "What happened to Diki?"

"The airport people got curious about their locked-up toilet. They found Diki before he woke up. Police came and Diki went—off to the local *calabozo*."

Cay swore. In French, like a lady.

Hodd got the drift. "I agree. I hung around the jail to make sure he was salted away. For twenty pesos the turnkey told me he'll stay salted till Monday morning, at least. Nothing much happens here on Sunday."

She paced the long room, thinking. She was still barefoot, but at Hodd's cautious knock she had flung on her negligee of deep-green silk. It was sleeveless but with a short cape that covered her shoulders; three buttons held it fastened across her stomach, and the rest was left to skill. Her thighs appeared through the silken folds whenever she paced by Hodd, and he would politely avert his eyes. He unwrapped a fresh stick of gum and said, "I followed through as far as I dared."

"I realize that. Your news isn't all bad, George. I think Diki was operating on his own, attacking me. We know he didn't have time to contact anyone else. So if he's out of circulation... well, perhaps we can find Valdes before Monday. Until Diki is turned loose, Valdes won't know I'm in town."

"It's a big town to comb. Fifty thousand, anyway."

"The depots will still be open. Airport, and try the bus lines to neighboring villages, and the Mexican Southern Pacific has a terminal here."

"Already checked the airport. Valdes hasn't left by plane."

Cay gave him a rewarding smile. "Also cover the hotels. And the tourist air and travel agencies may be open tomorrow. Banks will have to wait until Monday. So will the telephone company, and light and power— in case he's rented a house here. I've already looked in the hotel phone book. What'll stick us is if he's staying with friends. But we can try the camera shops to see if he's bought movie film... Here, divide some of this routine up."

"You're the boss," Hodd said. After making some meticulous entries in his pocket notebook, he left her.

Alone she swiftly donned fresh underclothes and a black linen dress, bare-armed, high-necked. She left her legs bare also and slipped her feet into high-heeled clogs with broad black straps.

Regretfully she pinned up her conspicuous hair and wrapped it completely in a polka-dot beach bandanna, even swathing the bangs on her forehead. The result was pleasingly piratical. After darkening her brows and lashes, Cay concluded she might get by as a very pale Mexican. At least she wouldn't appear incandescent in a crowd. And she knew that, after a few more conversations, she would have the *mazatleco* accent down pat.

With gun, tourist card, and pesos fitted into her black box purse, she set out into the languorous night. A taxi dropped her downtown at the Parque Revolución just as the cathedral clock tolled ten. She caught some of the camera shops before they closed down their iron screens and then, leaving the rest till tomorrow, she returned to the Parque Revolución. The marble benches lining the tiled walks of the city's main *plazuela* were pinkish-brown and dedicated like tombstones; the one Cay chose allowed her to sit through the *cortesía de Luis Guillermo Hijar 1948*. Behind her the stark façade of the Palacio Federal watched as darkly as she did across the park to where a crowd was streaming forth from the fortress gates of the Palacio Municipal; the basketball game in the city hall's patio had just ended. For a while the pushcarts of the shrimp, oyster, and coconut vendors did a brisk business and then the crowd thinned. There was no sign of Valdes.

The *plazuela* drowsed under its laurel trees. A jukebox still played fitfully from the refreshment bar beneath the bandstand; to the north of the bandstand's filigreed cupola reared the orange and blue spires of the cathedral, so high that their two neon crosses seemed to swim among the stars. The top-heavy busses vanished to their garages, the slurring scuff of huaraches and the clip-clop of horse carts died away. A khaki-clad policeman, armed with pistol and loaded swagger stick, eyed Cay thoughtfully, and when the cathedral clock struck midnight she somberly got up and walked back to her hotel.

She was showering again when, like an echo of her own brooding, she heard Hodd's voice say, "No luck." She whirled—but his voice had spoken to her down the air shaft. She reached up and knocked three times on the open transom to signify she'd understood. Between the cool sheets of the single bed, she fell asleep concocting further plans for the hunt.

Early next morning she set Hodd to watching masses at the cathedral. Still wearing the black linen frock and polka-dot bandanna, she breakfasted in the baronial dining room of the Hotel Belmar and then resumed her search on the hard leather seat of an *araña*. This kind of tiny black gig, with flat fringed roof and drawn by one small horse, seemed the most popular and inexpensive transportation in Mazatlán. Cay shrewdly chose one with a semblance of rubber on its two great wheels; to the driver's growing bewilderment she directed him back and forth through the Sunday silence of the city, exploring every street. Occasionally she dismounted into the blazing sunlight to investigate a cantina or patio café, or to converse with a sidewalk vendor or a street sweeper. She learned nothing... and with tomorrow's release of Diki, her search would be made doubly dangerous. She ate the main meal of the day, the *comida corrida,* at an ancient restaurant on Calle Sixto Osuna, and then discovered that the entire overheated populace had retired indoors for siesta. Only the black buzzards kept vigil, soaring circling omens in the blue-white sky.

At last the mustached *araña* driver eyed his strange passenger wearily. "Is there not some place of interest we could visit where my sorrowful beast may rest for a few moments only? A view of the lighthouse, perhaps, or our lovely cemetery, or the *corrida de toros?*"

"*Corrida de toros?*" Cay sat upright, seizing his arm. "Here in Mazatlán? At the hotel I was assured the nearest arena was three hundred miles away, in Guadalajara."

"Bah, they don't know everything, these hotels! Mazatlán may not observe the spectacle of the bulls with regularity, but at this very moment, in the arena on Calzada Gabriel Leyva Norte, progresses a benefit for the school of—"

"You must take me there immediately! No—first to the hotel."

At the Freeman, she slipped a hasty note under Hodd's door, praying he'd return soon: "Bullfight after all! Calzada G. Leyva N. Cover me." Cay realized she was perhaps too elated at the resurrection of this lead that her earlier information had forced her to discard. But the elusive Valdes was a Spaniard; she had originally discovered him through a bullfight in Tijuana; as an *aficionado* of both bulls and cameras, he must surely be unable to resist a look at Mazatlán's *corrida*.

The *araña* bounced her across the city again, through its outskirts of thatched and tin-roofed shanties, stately palms and motherly papaya trees standing sentry for the poor. Cay impulsively pressed a fifty-peso note into her driver's hand for his brilliant suggestion of the bullfight. It was also a thank offering to the goddess of chance. The rickety horse trotted along the endless causeway across mud flats and estuaries of the bay; Cay saw an old walled cemetery and a hill of army barracks, but no stadium hove into view.

"Have you more speed?" she asked, fidgeting. "The afternoon passes."

"It is not necessary. Please see ahead—the *corrida de toros.*"

Cay's heart sank. "Mother of God!" she murmured. "Do *mazatlecos* dare to term this a bullfight?" For within the scrubby grove of cottonwood trees rose no high-tiered commercial arena, but merely a split-rail corral surrounded by a gay throng of Mexicans who blocked her view.

"A parish fiesta. But there are bulls," rationalized the driver meekly. "Skillful bulls, since they are never allowed to be killed. However, if the generous lady doesn't foresee excitement enough—"

"I am here, so I shall look. Have the goodness to wait. Later we shall discuss this subject further." At a gate in the barbed-wire fence she paid a peso and fifty centavos admission to a matronly Mexican esconced behind a card table. Within the larger enclosure she elbowed her way through the crowd until she was standing by the rail fence.

Cay told herself that Valdes would never attend this *pachanga,* this whistle-stop exhibition—never. The *toreros* in the dusty corral were merely dungareed adolescents, scampering playfully between the horses of a half-dozen *vaqueros* in straw sombreros, who cantered around the ring, jesting with the spectators and swinging their *reatas* proudly. From an adjoining pen two men on foot belabored with stout clubs the hindquarters of an old bull, one of four.

The bull made a sudden bound into the corral, raising a shout from the spectators, but then he stood placidly considering his determined enemies. He was dull of horn and wise of eye; aside from his bulk, he looked anything but ferocious.

The youthful matador in a faded but conventional costume of purple and orange stepped forward boldly and flapped his tarnished gold cape for the bull's attention. From the far side of the corral the three-piece band struck up a rollicking air. After further consideration, the old bull lunged forward playfully. The matador scrambled aside wildly, drawing another delighted shout from the crowd. The bull stopped to survey all these noisy people; he seemed to shrug.

Cay could only smile sadly. Another time she might have enjoyed this simple earthbound spectacle. But not today, not without Valdes. With a perfunctory glance around, she prepared to turn away. And then she saw him.

Opposite her, a high narrow platform had been built to overhang the corral fence. One end of the platform was supported by the bole of a cottonwood tree, and at this end sat the band, the tuba player actually straddling the tree's crotch. The raised platform held some castoff chairs and benches, choice seats for those who came early.

No *aficionado* herself, Cay would never understand the forces that had caused Eduardo Valdes to secure an early seat at this affair. But there he sat in mid-air, his movie camera to his eye, eager for action below. Cay sucked in her breath, making a savage hissing sound. She withdrew slightly behind a fence post and, eying the quarry she had stalked so long, she felt her forehead burn feverishly in the shape of its disfiguring scar.

Valdes, who knew the Trader...

He hadn't changed so much in five years. He looked a bit plumper in his white suit and probably there were fewer oily curls beneath his Panama hat, but his dark sunken-cheeked face was the kind that never changed, not even in death.

A tiny hand grabbed Cay's. *"El toro! El toro!"* squealed a ragged little boy, pointing excitedly. The bull had found a loose rail and was shouldering his way out of the corral to join the audience. People scurried away, amid screams and shouts, and the *vaqueros* galloped lazily after the escaped beast, *reatas* poised.

Cay retreated, taking the little boy with her. She wasn't afraid of a mere bull, but the sudden exodus from the fence had left her exposed to Valdes' gaze if he should glance that way. She was glad of her foresight in covering her shining hair. She seated herself in the shade of a huge canopy hung within the barbed-wire enclosure. A feast was being prepared here to follow the entertainment. She bought some orange soda for herself and the boy, and loitered among the tables, waiting for Valdes to leave. The shadows were lengthening; he wouldn't be able to use his camera much longer.

As soon as the bull, festooned with ropes, was dragged helplessly back into the corral, Valdes buckled his camera into its carrying case. He rose and picked his way gingerly along the high platform toward the steps. Cay turned abruptly and joined in conversation with the women at their cooking. She gave Valdes a full two minutes to make the roadside gate and then, trembling with impatience, followed after him.

But seeing Valdes again only turned her frantic with frustration. He was handing a large bill to an *araña* driver—*her* driver, the only transportation in sight— and swinging up to the seat. She wanted to rush into the road, shout her protests at fate, hold Valdes back until she had an opportunity to follow.

But there was no opportunity. The *araña* was fifty yards away now, rolling at a trot. The driver, feeling guilty about the bullfight's lack of magnificence, fearing perhaps for the exorbitant fee she had already paid him, had allowed himself to be bribed.

Cay stood flat-footed and watched Valdes' back disappear down the causeway toward Mazatlán. She could feel the tears of rage on her cheeks.

Chapter Five

Sunday, December 2, 5:00 P.M.

Some of the Mexicans were regarding Cay's obvious distress with curiosity. Summoning her most pleading smile, Cay singled out an affluent-looking gentleman and headed toward him. She intended to ask for a bicycle or a horse or even a telephone to call a taxi.

But before she could speak, brakes squealed on the highway behind her. Then came a piercing whistle, and from the back window of a shabby blue Chevrolet, George Hodd beckoned to her. To the affluent Mexican's dismay, she whirled and ran for the road. Her knees weak with hope, she scrambled through the door Hodd was holding open.

"Miss Morgan, I just spotted him!" Hodd said, considerably excited for him. "Got your note, I just passed an *araña* back there, and who should be riding in it but—"

"I know," she panted. "I found Valdes and then lost him. Get this taxi going! Go right by him." She slid to the floor, out of sight but still talking. "Tell me when it's safe. There's a big intersection coming up, with a police sentry box. I saw a vacant *araña* there. If it's still there, I'll take that and tail Valdes when he comes along. This taxi would be too conspicuous shadowing a horse and buggy, so you keep way back—but handy for any showdowns."

"You're safe," Hodd said. Cay popped up onto the seat again and peered out the rear window. Valdes was no longer in sight on the causeway. Hodd tapped her arm. He said dubiously, "I don't know what you have in mind when you say showdown, Miss Morgan, but—"

She laughed excitedly. "I realize my pagan tendencies frighten you, George, but I really don't intend to kidnap him right here on the open road. I'm sorry I can't, but Mazatlán does have a police force and I shouldn't care to be locked up with Diki—not again. Don't worry, I merely want to confer with Valdes quietly." Which was a half-truth.

At the intersection of Calzada Leyva and Avenida Angela Peralta stood a lemon-colored kiosk, Caseta de Policía No. 3. By the curb lingered a black *araña* whose driver came fully awake at the sight of Cay's peso notes. However, she did not present him with any in advance. Hodd and his driver parked a quarter mile down the road, where the first vestiges of Mazatlán's residential section began.

Cay waited for nearly fifteen minutes in a ramshackle produce stand before Valdes' *araña* came rolling by. It turned west beneath the slender pines of the divided Avenida Peralta, apparently intending to return to the city by the roundabout seaside route. Cay signaled to Hodd, boarded her own *araña*, and instructed her driver to follow at a discreet distance.

Soon the leisurely pursuit began to gnaw at her confidence. Not that Valdes ever looked back or displayed the least suspicion; rather, from his meandering course and his driver's conversational gestures toward the reed-bound lagoons, he appeared to be going nowhere at all. Cay groaned, reining in her impatience. The Spanish pawnbroker might behave like a sight-seer, but, like the pelicans winging over the marshes, he would have to light sometime. Now and then she caught a glimpse of Hodd's taxi. He was paralleling her course, wherever possible, on hilly side streets to the south.

Five-thirty; the sun rested nearly on the horizon as she reached the red-cragged ocean shore; here, abruptly, began the Paseo Olas Altas with its smooth stretch of beach and sudden façade of civilization. Cay clenched her fists in exasperation as she saw Valdes carelessly trundling along the esplanade, toward the Hotel Freeman. She wondered if irony was leading him to her own door. Among the girders of the Freeman's uncompleted top story buzzards roosted ominously, waiting as she did.

But Valdes continued south on the curving boulevard and his *araña* began the climb of Cerro del Vigía, Lookout Hill, which guarded the harbor mouth. Cay halted her carriage until Hodd's taxi pulled alongside. "Wait for me at the hotel," she told him. "There aren't enough roads on that hill for this parade."

Halfway up Cerro del Vigía the walled residences dwindled away, leaving the upper slopes to sagebrush and gnarled pine trees. One of the highest homes stood gloomily uninhabited, a fire-gutted Tudor mansion. Beyond this the streets gradually merged into a single graveled scenic drive circling the bluffs at the tip of the city's peninsula.

Rounding a loop of road, Cay again came in view of her former *araña* and driver, halted by the cliff edge. Valdes was gone. But a path led down over the lip of the bluff to one of the many *glorietas*, small semicircular balconies, that studded this side of the peninsula.

"Pass on," Cay commanded her driver. "I will enjoy the view from the next *glorieta*." She turned her face away, hoping she wouldn't be recognized by Valdes' driver. Apparently she wasn't; his eyes were drowsily watching an approaching bicyclist.

Anxiously, Cay dismounted a hundred feet farther on and hurried down the ramp of another *glorieta*. These balustraded balconies of stone, man's addition to nature's erratic rock formations, had been built solely for the contemplation of nature's awesomeness. Far below raged the white-faced angry surf; westward lay the golden sheet of the Pacific, stretching to the very rim of the sun. But Cay could see nothing from the first rectangular platform. A jut of rock blocked her view of the neighboring *glorieta*, which Valdes presumably occupied. Valdes... and who else? She thought surely that he had come to this lonely place for a rendezvous. She scrambled down the steps to the next lower balcony.

She drew back against the rough cliffside, descending no farther. Now she could see Valdes. He stood on the bottommost platform of his *glorieta*, hands clasped behind his rump, looking out at the sea as if he owned it. Cay swallowed a cry of disappointment. Valdes was alone. He was simply watching the sun go down.

Seeking solace, Cay squinted at her wrist watch. Not quite six o'clock; perhaps the theoretical appointment was for six sharp. She waited. Valdes perched his camera case on the waist-high balustrade and ceremoniously lit a cigar. Smoke wreathing his head, he turned—to look up and across to where she stood.

"Señorita," he called with a smile.

Cay went rigid. But there was no obliterating her presence; her face and arms gleamed too palely in the dimming sunlight. To retreat would have been to admit her interest in him. So she played stranger, glancing down his way scornfully, then gazing off toward the ocean.

Valdes made her a gay little bow. "Don't pretend,

please," he said. "I know you're there just as you know I'm here. Have you enjoyed our pointless excursion, pet?"

Her choked throat wouldn't have allowed her to reply even had she been able to think of the words.

Valdes chuckled in that liquid way she remembered. "Yes, I am aware. Moreover, I believe I'm even aware of who you are, pet. Or who you were five years ago…" With an indolent wave he turned away to admire the last red streaks of the sunset.

Through the shock of surprise, Cay's brain sorted out vague ideas. She found herself unsnapping her purse, extracting her gun. To her right a brushy ledge of rock made a precarious path nearly to Valdes' *glorieta*. Then one long step over space and she could gain the platform above his, blocking his ascent. The drivers on the road overhead could not see either of them and were probably dozing. Perhaps with a gun in his plump back, Valdes would change his insultingly airy attitude to a more informative mood.

But before she could move, she heard a faint sound below, a musical chiming like a fairy tune. Valdes heard it too and spun around to face something behind him, something out of sight to Cay.

A shadow—in the fast fading light that was all she could make out, the arm shadow striking like a snake at Valdes' vest pocket, the tiny knife shadow withdrawing and vanishing.

Then the only movement on the *glorieta* was the white-suited form of Valdes. His outflung arms knocked his camera off the balustrade into space. When his hands returned to his chest, he staggered and buckled slowly to the stone floor of the balcony. He made no cry and, finally, no movement.

For the second time that afternoon Cay stood helpless, watching her priceless quarry slip away from her. But this time Eduardo Valdes had gone where she could not follow.

Chapter Six

Sunday, December 2, 6:00 P.M.

A moment later Cay had vanished from her *glorieta;* only her high-heeled clogs and her purse lay in a shadowy corner of the balustrade. But a chance watcher from the rumbling sea below might have gazed upward at a curious sight. Across the scowling face of the cliff there crept, step by step, a barefoot woman in a modish black frock, its skirt held high on her shapely legs. The same hand that kept her skirt free of her legs carried a pearl-handled revolver. The ledge was narrow; as she advanced carefully, Cay leaned her body toward the cliff, her free hand constantly maintaining a grasp on the flimsy brush and roots that sprouted from between the sheer rocks. No fear glimmered in her intent eyes—even during that tortured moment when she was forced to round a fat sprawling cactus to which she didn't dare cling—and when the rough ledge came to a precipitous end, she made a short leap to the railing of the other *glorieta*.

A quick look around, pistol ready, assured her that

she was alone. The shadow killer of Valdes had not lingered. This *glorieta* was bordered on one side by a thick growth of sagebrush through which descended a steep but usable dirt path. Now she could understand how the knifer had reached Valdes without being seen by either her or the victim. But she could not understand the strange soft chiming she had heard immediately before the murder.

Cay padded down the cold stairs to the lower balcony where the dead body lay. The skull face stared upward at her and the first faint traces of stars in the sky. She bent and commenced ransacking the pockets of the white suit, regretting only that this dead lump of flesh under her prying hands represented the probable failure of her plans. How was she to find the Trader without Valdes?

As she searched for some scrap of information that might rescue her mission of vengeance, she fastidiously avoided the wound in Valdes' chest. Surgically neat, it had bled scarcely at all. Just below the breastbone, apparently an upward thrust into the heart itself. The assassin knew his business.

Who? She wondered if the Trader had killed Valdes, for some reason of his own. Then she shook her head slowly at that theory. The Spanish pawnbroker had been the Trader's trusted aide for many years. And the circumstances—so open to chance, almost impulsive... Did the Trader have another enemy in Mazatlán besides herself?

She found the letter in Valdes' brassbound wallet; it was all she found of any value to her. It was typewritten in English. The envelope was gone, so there was no telling where it had been mailed, but it was dated less than two weeks before. Holding it close in the gathering dusk, she read: "My dear Eduardo: As outlined in previous note, events have bettered. Our concluding arrangements must be made by 9 December. Your presence in Mazatlán before that time I consider vital, certainly, and I shall leave it to you to summon Diki or one of the others similarly talented. Let me impress upon you—by no means underestimate the size and urgency of this coup. Until that happy day—"

It was signed with a penciled "T."

Cay pressed the letter between her hands for a moment before she tucked it in her dress pocket. She had never before handled anything that she knew had been touched by the Trader. The letter was a link between them. She was getting nearer. The tone of the message left no doubt in her mind; the Trader himself was in Mazatlán or nearby. He intended to accomplish something by December ninth, next Sunday. That he had summoned Valdes and Diki and perhaps others gave exciting indication that sizable profits were involved in his mysterious project. Although his illicit enterprises reached to most parts of the world, the Trader involved as few persons as possible in each transaction. It was safer that way.

Cay rose to her feet, unwilling to leave Valdes when she'd learned so little, but fearing that her *araña* driver might come in search of his passenger. And there remained the risky ledge to recross before the light got any worse. But, remembering the motion-picture camera, she glanced curiously over the balustrade from where it had fallen toward the noisy surf below.

Curiosity had its reward. The strap of the camera's case had hooked on a sagebrush limb about a yard below the broad railing. Conscious of the hastening moments, Cay leaned over the balustrade on her stomach. Reaching down as far as she could without losing her balance, she painstakingly fished the camera up again.

She paused to perform one last act, for which she had brought her lipstick in her dress pocket. She knelt beside Valdes and drew a large red T on his forehead.

The ledge across the cliff seemed even narrower in the gloom, and the stolen camera slung from her shoulder knocked about uncomfortably. But she regained her own *glorieta* without discovery. Brushing off her feet, she slipped into her clogs and replaced gun and lipstick in her purse as she trotted up the steps to the roadway.

Her driver had lighted the twin oil lanterns on his *araña*. He clucked in relief as she appeared out of the night. "Ay, señora, another moment and I would have come in search of you."

"I was entranced by the quality of the sunset and the waves," Cay told him, congratulating herself on her timing. She climbed up through the back of the gig, and when the seat had been folded down behind her she said, "I became frightened with the dark. No doubt I'm foolish, but I imagined that other eyes were watching me. A man, perhaps…" She let it dangle like a question.

The driver laughed gallantly, turning his horse. "That is an experience to which a woman such as you must have grown accustomed. But tonight, no."

"Then no one passed you on the road?"

"No one." He hesitated, and Cay wondered if he had noticed her acquisition of a movie camera during her visit to the *glorieta*. "Unless, of course, you refer to the bicyclist."

Cay tried to recall. Just before their halt at the *glorieta*, someone had bicycled by the *araña*. But she had been concentrating too hard on the pursuit of Valdes to notice any details. And although her driver had spoken of the bicyclist in the masculine gender, she soon found that he wasn't positive the rider had been man, woman, or child. "In the dazzle of the sunset, señora…"

Rolling downhill toward the lights of the Paseo Olas Altas, they passed Valdes' *araña*, the driver fast asleep but waiting. This time he obviously had not been paid beforehand. Cay wondered how soon he would go looking for his passenger.

Chapter Seven

Sunday, December 2, 7:00 P.M

She turned on the shower and let it run, though she was still fully dressed and intended to remain that way. With her head close to the air shaft transom, she commenced whistling loudly, a full chorus of "Come, All

Ye Faithful." In less than a minute, Hodd was rapping at her door.

Slowly chomping his gum, he watched her brush traces of cliff dust from her black frock. "Valdes?" he asked.

"Dead."

He stopped chewing and his wooden face stared at her.

"Well, go on, say it," she snapped. "Leave it to a woman and so forth."

"I wasn't thinking that. Not in your case."

"Damn it, I didn't kill him. He's no use to me dead." She told him what had happened and flung him the letter she had taken from the dead man. "At least, I know we're on the right track."

Hodd didn't comment as he read the letter through.

Cay said, "Notice the date he mentions, December ninth. Next Sunday is a deadline of some sort for him. After that, he may be going somewhere else. I don't think I could stand to lose him again."

Hodd turned the paper over and asked, "What's all this?" and Cay saw what she hadn't noticed on the dim *glorieta*. Someone had lightly penciled a series of figures on the paper, financial calculations apparently. The sums told her nothing, but she was staggered at their size; they ran to seven and eight figures.

"I'd guess," she said softly, "that this represents the coup the Trader told Valdes not to underestimate. Scarcely believable, but…" She produced the movie camera. The initials E. V. were stamped on its case in gold. "Here, we haven't time for speculation. There's a slim chance that Valdes may have photographed something besides today's bullfight. Some scenery or something that'll narrow down our search for wherever he's been staying. You find someone who can develop this film, rent us a projector, and—"

"Don't forget this is Sunday night," he warned. "The town's locked up tight."

"I didn't hire you for reasons why not. You'll find a large camera shop on Calle Angel Flores. There's a number in the window to call in case of emergency. I consider this an emergency."

He gazed down at her bleakly as he slung the camera over his shoulder. He adjusted his hat on his bald head, hesitating as if about to tell her something. He decided not to.

Cay asked suddenly, "Do I frighten you, George?"

"No. People never frighten me. Sometimes consequences do."

After he'd gone she poured herself a small brandy. The trouble with Hodd, she thought, was that he couldn't comprehend a whole woman. Like most men, he could see women only in the half role of passivity, never as positive or active factors. Men liked women they could call "Baby," which epitomized their view of womankind as something charming but inferior. Cay emitted a dainty snarl. Baby, servant, tool of desire; these represented femininity to all the Hodds in the world. She knew Hodd resented working for a woman; she guessed that he salved his pride by not thinking of her as a woman at all, but as a freak.

With her second brandy, Cay speculated dreamily on what it would be like to give herself to a man; not just her pretty body, but her entire precious self. Not

to a Hodd, of course, but to one of the rare other kind
of man. Not in trade, or with any scheme in mind, but
freely to give in every sense, allow her *self* to be mastered. Be mastered, but remain mistress. She speculated until she shivered with a phantom desire. Then
she sighed wearily, unaccountably feeling the weight
of years upon her. What hope for what future? Give
freely? That'll be the day, she thought harshly.

Having no appetite for dinner, she switched off the
lights in her room and lounged in the canvas chair on
her dark balcony. She sipped now and then at her
brandy and used her binoculars to watch the promenade along the sea wall. About nine o'clock there
occurred a stir of traffic on Olas Altas; a police panel
truck rushed by the Freeman, followed by an official
sedan. They disappeared up the hilly road of Cerro del
Vigía. Cay smiled thinly. The murder of Valdes had
been reported at last. She swung her chair around and
waited for the police to reappear.

Nearly an hour later the panel truck and sedan
came back down the hill at a slower pace. She trained
the binoculars on them, but it was too dark to pene-
trate their windows. Suddenly she sprang to her feet,
fingers gripping tightly on the glasses.

By chance she had focused for an instant on the
shadows of an uncompleted apartment house at the
foot of the hill. The headlights of the truck swept
momentarily across the face of a man lurking there,
revealing his slant eyes and yellow hair and the white
scarf hung about his neck.

Her glimpse was brief, barely a flash of recognition,
and when the lights of the following sedan illuminated

the same spot, Diki the stranger had vanished. So he was out of jail. Cay abandoned the half-born notion of pursuit. The odds against her were too great. When she resumed her seat on the balcony, her revolver lay in her lap.

The next slow hours passed without incident. She dozed occasionally, between glances at her wrist watch, and presently she shared the warm Mexican night only with the throbbing surf. She came awake after three o'clock, hearing lonely footsteps on the sidewalk below. She was waiting beside her door when the knock came. It was Hodd.

He gave the gun in her hand a worried look. "Don't you have anything to take for your nerves?" In addition to Valdes' camera he also was carrying a weighty black case, a motion-picture projector.

"My nerves don't bother me," said Cay, bolting the door behind him. "But Diki does. He's out of jail early."

Hodd grunted when she told him the details. "Tough break, but can't be helped. There's no way for two Americans to pull a twenty-four-hour stake-out on a Mexican jail without being noticed. Maybe I can track him down anyway."

They set up the projector on the desk, focusing it against the bare stucco wall over the head of her bed. The sixteen-millimeter film was a hundred-foot reel, but only half of it, Hodd explained, had been exposed. "Meaning Valdes probably loaded up fresh before going to the bullfight."

"I'm not expecting anything." Cay pulled the drapes across the open balcony doors and flipped off the lights again. "But it couldn't be passed up."

The little *pachanga* began to live again, flickeringly, in a rectangle on the wall. The film contained nothing but the bullfight, the only point of interest for Cay being Cay herself, distantly in the background of a couple of shots. Neither of them said anything for a while after the reel had whirred its way through the machine. Hodd finally muttered, "Well, that's that, I guess," and reversed the projector's action. On the wall, the bullfight began leaping backward.

As the reel reached its beginning once more, Cay straightened suddenly from her slumped position on the bed. "Run that again!" she commanded, and when Hodd had done so she said, "Something at the start, just a flash. Did you catch it?"

Hodd was examining the ribbon of celluloid with his flashlight. "Yeah, just two frames. Valdes must have shot out his leader tape on something else and got a piece on the film proper." Patiently he rethreaded the reel and jockeyed the machine forward and in reverse until the picture they wanted was frozen on the wall.

Cay saw nothing familiar. In the background was the veranda of a dark house, apparently the home of some well-to-do family, and probably located nearby, for tropical vines entwined its pillars. Someone indistinguishable even as to sex lounged in the veranda's shade. However, there was another person in the picture, a man's profile near to the camera, his pointed features limned by bright sunlight. It was a rather fox-like face with a long upper lip, dark bushy hair, and spectacles with thick black rims.

Cay thought, It can't be the Trader. Surely he wouldn't let his picture be taken.

Hodd let the film move on. "Ever see Goggles before?"

"No, he's new to me. But I'll know him from now on."

"Looked American to me. What did you make of the house?"

"Apparently where Valdes was holed up. Looked big, expensive. No verandas in the city, so it must be someone's country house. We've only got till next Sunday, but we ought to be able to spot Goggles or the house by then, one or both."

"Ought to. We were lucky to get this film developed so quickly."

"Wherefore rejoice?" asked Cay conversationally. But a set look had come over her face. "What conquest brings he home? What tributaries follow him to Rome, to grace in captive bonds his chariot wheels...?"

Hodd stared at her as if she'd gone mad. Cautiously, Cay eased herself off the bed, her hand reaching toward the pistol on the chiffonier. Still reciting in casual tones, she pointed the gun toward the heavy draperies that screened the balcony.

Hodd didn't avoid trouble when it came visiting, and he was quick on his feet. He hurled himself in a straight line for the drapes. The word he growled between his teeth was "Diki."

Chapter Eight

Monday, December 3, 4:00 A.M.

Hodd's charge billowed the drapes wildly. By the time Cay and her gun could follow to the balcony, the scuffling noises had ceased. But the man whom Hodd half thrust, half carried into the room was not Diki.

Cay turned on the lights and eyed the man coldly. Although his arms were pinioned by Hodd, the stranger—a Mexican—smiled at her and inclined his head graciously. No one spoke. The whirring projector ran out of film and the loose end of celluloid began flapping round and round excitedly. Without taking her gaze from the intruder, Cay hooked the electric cord with her heel and unplugged it from the wall socket.

The tail of the man's red shirt hung partly outside his knife-creased trousers, his extravagant necktie was disarranged, and a pair of sunglasses was nearly falling from his shirt pocket. He wore no coat or hat. He was short, plump, with a round face like a brown biscuit; his cavalier mustache and slicked-back hair looked as neat as black paint. What lovely teeth! thought Cay detachedly as she patted over his pockets. The Mexican gave a smiling sigh, as if in ecstasy at her touch. She scowled at him and told Hodd, "No gun."

"Of what use are weapons to me?" exclaimed their

prisoner in accented English. He popped his eyes scornfully at the revolver in Cay's hand. "When one has wits, nothing else is—"

"Since I seldom feel witty at this hour of morning, I'll just hold onto my gun," said Cay. "You might try explaining how your big brain led you to my balcony!"

"I might try, *huera*, but—"

"Kindly do not address me as 'blondie,' señor."

"As to that, you'd know best. But I lose my head from this excruciating pain in my arm. I grow dizzy, my words falter... Eh?"

"Let him go, George." Hodd released him but stood close.

"Blessed relief," said the Mexican, rolling his shoulders and flexing his plump hands. His fingers sparkled with jeweled rings. After making his clothes neat he said, "You wish to know me, of course." He made a full bow to Cay, which caused his dark glasses to fall from his pocket to the floor; he retrieved them before straightening. "Your servant, señora, has the honor to be Rómulo María Felix, of Ciudad Mexico. Of the profession of detective. You don't smile?"

"Utter rot," said Cay.

With a flourish, Felix presented his card. Beneath the name and Mexico City address was the legend: *"Servicios Extraordinarios—Pronto! Confidential! Económico!"*

"Oh, a *private* detective!" exclaimed Cay, and then couldn't help laughing at the disgusted expression on Hodd's face.

"A specialist," admitted Felix, "in the extramarital lark." He looked from one to the other of his captors, his big eyes rolling slyly. "Hence my professional interest in you two persons who have been playing about in this hotel room all night. I doubt you are married—to each other."

Hodd said, "I've yet to meet a divorce detective who doesn't make my skin crawl."

"You generalize, Señor George. However, I forgive your rash tongue." Genially he turned, extending his hand. As Hodd stood gaping at the Mexican's effrontery, Felix kicked him in the groin. Hodd sank to his knees, doubled over with pain, his mouth wide in soundless agony.

Cay ground the muzzle of her gun against Felix's spine. "Easy, or you get yourself blown in two!"

Felix slowly revolved to face her, grinning insolently. "You don't dare shoot me, *huera,* not at the moment. What I have done, I have done to advise you people that I don't enjoy careless handling. Nor do I enjoy threats from a woman, however beautiful." With his thumbs he smoothed down his mustache. "Dispose of the gun, eh, *huera?*"

"You're right." Cay grinned and stepped back. "Shooting you would make too much noise. You're right that far." Still grinning, she whipped the pistol barrel against Felix's cheekbone. The force of the blow set him down on the bed, his slashed cheek dripping blood onto his shirt.

"George," said Cay sharply. "You're in his debt too."

Hodd was already on his feet, thin lips still clamped tight in pain. Flushed with anger, he wiped the perspiration from his bald head. Felix tried to slip aside as Hodd's left hand hooked in the front of his red shirt, anchoring him for the right, which knocked him sprawling on the tiled floor.

Cay said, "A lovely blow, George." With her gun alert to tricks, she searched Felix's limp body; papers in his wallet bore out the identity he claimed.

The contents of the water carafe brought Felix around. He sat on the floor, investigating his head with ring-laden fingers, patting his split cheek with a snowy handkerchief while the other two watched him silently. Finally he looked up at Cay with a pained burlesque of a smile.

"*Ay de mi,*" he groaned. "Señora, I underrated you dreadfully."

"Then why did you come at all?"

"To listen, of course. I am a great student of eavesdropping. You made such cryptic conversation about a certain veranda and a certain man whom you quite aptly called Goggles."

"And what do you call him?"

"The name Señor Goggles will serve, won't it?" He paused tantalizingly. "For those who do not know better, I mean."

Hodd said, "Stow that hogwash and tell us how you got on the lady's balcony, mister."

"How? Easily." Felix pulled a ring of keys from his trousers pocket. "The room adjoining is unoccupied. The personal keys of Rómulo María Felix will open any door in Mexico."

"When I say how, I mean why, what for," growled Hodd. "Speak up."

"Why is as simple as how. Over XERJ, the local radio, I heard them tell of Señor Eduardo Valdes, who died with a scarlet T on his forehead. A very interesting disease that sounds like." He grinned and nodded up at their impassive faces. "Yes, indeed. Since I am close to the hearts of the police, and also curious about the late Valdes, I investigated. A strange fact developed. The *araña* driver testified that Valdes carried a motion-picture camera. But where was it? Not to be found at the scene. Hence when, in the early morning hours, I saw this American gentleman carrying not only a camera but also a projector for the viewing of film, I found my curiosity insatiable. I followed."

Hodd looked at Cay. "Not a bad story. Quick anyway."

Felix got to his feet, mopping his damp hair and neck. "So much water," he complained. "Brandy would have been kinder. Nevertheless, I am now ready to hear your side of the case, the outpourings of your hearts regarding your interest in—ah, Señor Goggles."

"I'm afraid that's not the way the script reads," said Cay. "You're *our* guest. What about Goggles? What about your knowing Valdes?"

"You have a singular lack of confidence," said Felix, pressing his handkerchief against his cheek. "None of us can flourish in an atmosphere of suspicion and distrust. I've put myself out being frank and open with you two ruffians. If you won't reciprocate, you leave me no choice but to put myself out—permanently." And he took a step toward the hall door.

Hodd got in his way. "Back up. You haven't got permission."

Felix smiled in his face. "I fear the resulting disturbance will now cause the police to be summoned. Those angry overworked police! For my part, I don't care. It's not I who possesses the dead man's missing camera or shows the dead man's motion pictures. But how much do you care?"

Hodd glanced worriedly at Cay.

She said softly, "I'm afraid he's right, George. We must let him go."

From the door Felix smiled and bowed at them. "Thank you for the enlightenment. Someday we may all laugh together. Until then, *huera*."

Hodd went to the door, making sure he was gone.

Cay said, "The camera and film go in the ocean. What about the shopkeeper who developed it?"

"He was sleepy. I didn't let him see the initials on the case. No use asking for trouble." Hodd thumbed in the direction of Felix' departure. "Unpleasant encounter, but I think we can write him off as a cheap operator, digging after nothing. I don't see that he knows anything."

Cay shook her head wearily. "No, the lad's clever. He practically set himself up to be caught tonight. He was sizing us up—maybe for himself, maybe for someone else. I wish I knew."

"We know this much: He saw us together. Now we're both spotted."

"But I'm not certain how bad that is. I'm beginning to think the Trader is having troubles of his own here in Mazatlán. Perhaps we've arrived in time for the big war." She met Hodd's eyes and forced a smile. "You don't like wars, George?"

"No, can't say that I do. Especially when I don't know who's fighting."

"We'll find out. Trust me."

"We may find out, but I won't promise the other." He left abruptly and she bolted the door angrily.

Chapter Nine

Wednesday, December 5, 2:00 P.M.

For two days Cay failed to locate the unknown Goggles or his vined veranda, although she and Hodd, separately, toured the back-country roads in ever widening arcs. Nor, despite her rash challenging of the Trader—the twice-scribbled T in red lipstick—did Jack Diki or anyone else come to seek her out, not even the flamboyant Rómulo María Felix. The days themselves seemed to conspire against her, melting away, hastening her toward the imminent deadline of the next Sunday, when she might lose what feeble clues she had.

Ever watchful, she felt the shivering excitement of being watched. This ominous feeling came to her most strongly along the Paseo Olas Altas, but her experienced eye could never distinguish anyone suspicious among the loiterers. At night she dreamed wildly of the eyes of the Trader himself, mockingly watching her from some secret place.

Wednesday afternoon, without warning, the break came.

Her taxi was headed away from Mazatlán along the eastern bay-girt side of the peninsula. Here the long concrete embankment of water front served as a secondary street for automobiles and *arañas,* which dodged among the donkey engines chuffing to and from warehouses. A forest of masts swayed gently along the edge of the concrete wharf, fishing boats of every size and description, plus the grimly looming sides of a gray Mexican gunboat. Gulls squawked and stevedores shouted.

Cay had seen, heard, and smelled it all before. Impatiently she fiddled with her flowered gloves as her taxi was held up by a truckload of shrimp. She hitched up her bodice, suddenly fretful that she had worn the topless dress today. But it was of white cotton and cool, a short cape of white lace covering her bare shoulders. A gleam of brass caught her idly roving eye and she looked at the big cabin cruiser, white and trim with rakish lines. Concha was the sleek craft's gilded name and… "God in Heaven!" breathed Cay.

Aft, on a canvas deck stool, sat Goggles. He munched a sandwich from the straw hamper at his feet. Middling in size and age, he was dressed in sporty blue, a fancy yachting cap perched on his bushy brown hair. Heavy-rimmed spectacles flashed in the sunlight as his face turned toward her.

She couldn't imagine that meek face as the Trader's. She didn't let herself be seen. When her taxi had zigzagged a hundred yards farther, she got out and dismissed it. Work and conversation ceased along the wharf as she strolled back toward the cruiser. Cay found time to be pleased with this tribute although her mind was busy sketching out a plan of attack. She had not covered her long hair and bangs today, and she knew that she gleamed like a silver peso in the sun.

She widened her smile, breathlessly expanded her breasts against the front of her dress as she sauntered down the gangplank to the afterdeck of the Concha, where Goggles sat watching her.

Goggles swallowed hard, bright brown eyes widening behind their lenses, and rose awkwardly to his feet. By this time Cay was near enough for him to smell the sandalwood. She flourished her gloves to make certain the rich scent of her reached him. She said, "Forgive me for not waiting to be invited, Captain, but a boat like this is exactly what I've been waiting for. What are your rates?"

He stared with astonishment.

She gave him a puzzled blink. "Rates, Captain. For fishing. You'll have to teach me from the ground up, but I'm a determined learner. My first requisite was a really clean boat, and this one certainly—"

"This? This isn't a fishing boat." He had a thin dry American voice. He was beginning to smile.

"No? Then what is it? Oh, never mind, Captain, I'll hire it anyway. Now don't tell me you're booked. Surely I can be squeezed in somewhere."

"This isn't for hire. It's mine—my private launch. I'm sorry."

She gazed at him with sweet disbelief. Goggles flushed and then she ducked her head. "Oh, damn," she muttered. "This is my day for being a fool." Smiling wryly, she said, "I'm the sorry one, Captain. Captain?"

"Just mister. Swan. Spencer Swan."

"I'm Cay Morgan, Cay for Catherine. Miss for— well, for missing brains, I guess." She gave him her fingers for an extra second not required by formality.

He said, "Oh, don't feel you looked foolish. Joke on both of us."

"Mind if I sit down for a moment?" She sank quickly into a low-slung deck chair where he could watch her rounded knees. "I've repented. I'm glad I was an idiot just to hear a mister talk instead of a señor. Do you make your home right here in Mazatlán, Mr. Swan?"

Spencer Swan didn't know quite what to do about her. "I was just eating my lunch," he said vaguely. Then, not wanting to appear ungracious, he added, "My hands are over at the warehouse, you see," and sat again on the canvas stool. He tried to stare at Cay but at the same time not look at her, the pearls on her ear lobes, her languorous posture in the low chair, her bare inviting knees, her gleaming hair.

"Your hands?" Cay chuckled. "You sound like an octopus."

"My workers. I raise coconuts. Had to come in for equipment. My island is off the coast, a little south of here. Isla de Puesta del Sol. If you don't speak Spanish—Sunset Island."

"Your own *island,* all yours?" Cay sat up straight, eyes sparkling. "Well, for heaven's sake!" No wonder neither she nor Hodd had been able to locate that veranda in the back country, all this time it had been sitting out in the Pacific Ocean. But she masked her excitement with a dreamy look, leaning slightly forward so that Swan would appreciate the twin curves at the top of her strapless dress. She was glad now that she had worn it. "Sunset Island, coconuts... And I thought romance was long dead. I've never seen a coconut plantation."

"Haven't you?" Swan didn't swallow the bait but he didn't reject it either. Somewhat like a fish, he swam around it. "Well, I don't know, Miss Morgan. You'd probably be disappointed. Probably it'd be just another graveyard of romance."

"That's very good. That's how I've felt about Mazatlán so far. But I've bothered you enough, Mr. Swan." She stretched lazily to her feet. "It's been wonderful talking to a fellow gringo."

This time she was glad to feel Swan tentatively prolonging the handclasp. Withdrawing her fingers, she gave him a sidelong half-embarrassed glance that implied: Please—we've barely met. Fortunately we've met, though... That hooked him.

He said, "No need to rush off, is there? I mean, if you haven't eaten, why don't you share a sandwich with me?" Then with a show of deprecation, "Neither I nor my sandwiches are any real bargain, but..."

He invited contradiction. Cay obliged him. If Eduardo Valdes had been staying or hiding on Swan's island, she was determined to see the place, preferably as a guest. Exactly what she would do with Swan, once she was alone with him on his island or in his house, she had no idea—but she wasn't there yet. As for villainy, he exhibited less than what she considered the male average. She ate one of his ham sandwiches and a juicy papaya, and drank lime juice from his thermos jug. During lunch he took three different pills, apologizing nervously as he did so. He was a rueful man with queer defenses; he seemed to anticipate adverse opinions about himself and tried to blunt them by expressing them first. Cay could play any game; by the end of lunch they were saying, "Yes, Cay," and "I wonder, Spencer."

While they ate, a pickup truck parked above on the concrete wharf. Two bare-chested Mexicans, the Concha's crew, carried long packing cases into the depths of the cruiser. Tarpaulin coverings prevented Cay from glimpsing any labels on the crates.

She guessed they contained rifles, and her heart beat a little faster. Silently she urged Swan to be quick with his invitation to visit his island.

He showed her the expensively fitted interior of the Concha. Hurry up, she thought, say *something*. She dawdled by the luxurious little bar and won herself a drink. She made her eyes innocent as she looked at him over the glass. She asked for a cigarette but abstained from using her holder for fear he might see the gun in her purse. The cigarette gave her another opportunity to touch his hand lightly. It was clammy, and with his drink he took still another pill.

Then she felt the floor quiver under her feet. She pretended she thought it was the drink, leaning against him and saying, "Spencer, I can usually hold my liquor, but I'm afraid this time—"

"It's the engines," he blurted out hastily. "Cay, don't think I'm trying to shanghai you or anything, but I thought if you'd care to have dinner with me on the island…" He took her hand. "Please don't be alarmed,

Cay. I meant to mention it before. You needn't worry about an old wreck like myself. Say you'll come. I know you'll enjoy the island, and I promise you I'll see that you get safely back to Mazatlán again."

She smiled deep into his eyes. "We're already under way, aren't we, Spencer?"

"Well—yes."

"I don't mind," she whispered, and let him hold her hand.

Chapter Ten

Wednesday, December 5, 5:00 P.M.

Ten miles south of Mazatlán and ten miles off the Mexican coast, the Isla de Puesta del Sol rose gently from the sea, a verdant bosomy mound. A broad sandy beach ringed its eight square miles, the silver setting of a tropic emerald.

"The south third—you can't see it from here—isn't cultivated yet," Swan told Cay as they cruised toward the short low pier. "My laziness or incompetence or something, I guess."

To Cay, the serried rows of coco palms, slender pale trunks loftily topped with feathery fronds, made the island look like a green pincushion stuck full of identical green hatpins. Swan shyly squeezed her hand; he hadn't given her any trouble on the short voyage and she felt toward him a sort of grateful contempt. However, she affectionately returned his pressure, meanwhile engrossed with the plantation house coming into view.

The pier, on the coastal side of the island, traversed the wide beach to a palm-shaded clearing where the house stood. Dark vertical planking, red tile roof—but it was the vined pillars of the encircling veranda that gave Cay a thrill of recognition. Valdes slept here, she reflected grimly. Why? She clutched her death-laden purse more tightly. Other guests might arrive yet tonight: Diki, Felix, the Trader... She was prepared.

Her pale blue eyes moved among the dark throng of workers, men and women, streaming down to meet the returning Concha. They came from the thatched shanties and tin-roofed storehouses east of Swan's house. They trudged along the narrow-gauge tracks that appeared from the palm forest and ran to the end of the pier. She saw a pair of rail carts, man-powered, standing idle in the late sunlight. More uneasily she noticed the vicious-edged machetes used for splitting coconuts; one of the heavy blades hung from the belt of every man. From tonight on they would be armed with rifles.

Spencer Swan was guarding something more valuable than coconuts. His life?

The cruiser bumped the pier. "*Oye, Spencer, aquí!* Give me a hand up!" It was the mellow voice of a woman, her English slurred. Cay spun around, startled, and Swan gave a little jump away from her side. But there was no one to be seen near at hand.

Swan mumbled, "Oh, good lord, I didn't see her in the water," and went over to the rail of the Concha. Cay followed and looked down at the upturned face and foreshortened body of a woman treading water alongside the white hull. She wore no bathing cap; her heavy black hair was coiled round her head in braids. She was Mexican and handsomely mature, with broad cheeks and dark glinting eyes, and a large red smile until she saw Cay.

Swan leaned down and, using both hands, gruntingly helped her walk up the side of the cruiser and across the rail. She didn't thank him. She said, "I didn't know of the visitor because you didn't telephone."

"Slipped my mind. You know my memory," said Swan awkwardly. "I happened to run into Cay Morgan, a friend of mine from the States. Cay, this is Concha, my wife."

"Concha, of course—like the boat," Cay said brightly. "Spencer's told me all about you." She wanted to laugh at this sudden piquant emergence of a wife. Concha Swan acknowledged the introduction coldly, and the women's gazes prowled over each other. Swan gained some respect in Cay's estimation. His tall wife, as slickly glistening as a dolphin in her brief black bathing suit, was a worthy conquest for any man. Squared shoulders, proud breasts, strongly curved hips, long and smoothly muscled thighs—a magnificent body over which descended slow droplets of water that fell to the deck.

Concha stated, "Then I must inquire of the dinner. Do believe that our house is yours, Miss Morgan." Shifting into rapid Spanish, she remarked to her husband, "What a stupid swine you are!" and crossed to the pier. She strode rapidly toward the house, her firm hips swaying angrily.

Cay and Swan followed more slowly. He seemed upset by his wife's behavior but, characteristically, avoided the subject. "...one of the guest rooms. I expect you'll want to shower. Heat's sticky today." They crossed the veranda into the cool dim reaches of the house, which seemed largely furnished in rattan.

"Spencer, darling, I'm in our room," Concha's voice floated along a wainscoted hallway.

He didn't answer. Cay was listening carefully but could hear no other person in the house. Swan showed her into an airy bedroom at the beginning of the hall. It was yellow-plastered, wainscoted, and with the usual bare tiled floor. Cay hadn't seen a carpet since arriving in Mazatlán.

"Well..." Swan fumbled around the doorway for a moment, expressing hopes for Cay's comfort, then suddenly seized her and pressed his cheek against her pearly hair. She submitted passively. "Well... at dinner, then," he stammered, and she shut him out with a melting smile. She discovered the door's lock was out of order.

She pulled the curtains across the French doors leading onto the veranda and wearily stripped off her clothes. "Oh, God," she muttered about nothing in particular. She allowed herself a few seconds' collapse on the bed, arms and legs and blonde tresses sprawled wide. She found it difficult to convince herself that she was getting any nearer to the Trader; she moodily fancied she was being swept away from him. The irate Concha and her halfhearted spouse were rather less than she had bargained for. She wanted a full-scale brush with the enemy, not a long evening in a jangled

but average household. Yet she was positive about
Swan's shipment of rifles, and his picture *had*
appeared on the film from Valdes' camera...

She got up and, stuffing a cigarette into her ivory
holder, stalked into the bathroom. She carried her
purse and gun with her. This door locked. She was
standing under the lukewarm shower, gingerly
smoking with wet fingers, when she heard the muted
sound of voices in argument. She cocked an ear to the
wall. She failed to make out any words but discovered
that the voices sounded stronger near the shower
pipes. Evidently the Swans were discussing her in their
own bathroom, the water pipes relaying a murmur.

Cay stubbed out her cigarette. Was this trip another
of her familiar dead ends? She was soaking wet but
determined to eavesdrop and couldn't spare time to
dry or dress.

The bath towel solved her problem. It was the
European variety, a vast area of thick coarse material.
When she draped it about her damp shoulders, it
enveloped her modestly to the shins. Leaving her
shower running in case the Swans were keeping tabs
on her location, she concealed her purse within the
folds of the towel and crept out into the hall.

Another room lay between her quarters and what
she supposed was the master bedroom. Ready with
her doors-so-much-alike excuse, she quickly let herself in. It was another bedroom like her own, and as
deserted. She made a beeline for the bathroom,
guessing that it adjoined the Swans'. Now, with her ear
against the wall of this shower stall, she could hear
quite clearly. Next door, Swan's voice mingled with the

water of the shower. His wife's voice came more clearly. Apparently Concha had followed him into the bathroom to continue an argument.

"...certain you can't," Concha was saying. "Voluptuous little thing. Be rid of her."

Cay bared her teeth ferociously.

Swan said, "Your jealousy astounds me, dear one. When I review your own actions of these recent weeks—"

"Jealousy, no. That died not so recently. Sleep with her in town if she represents your taste—but bringing her here endangers us all. I sense she suspects the island."

"I'm certain she does, she wanted so dearly to come," agreed Swan. Cay bit her lip; Spencer Swan wasn't so naïve as she had supposed. "But what's here for her to see? So close your mouth. Besides adding a bit of spice, I believe Señorita Morgan worth probing more deeply."

"Swine, swine without brains! You know she should be killed!"

"I decide what I know, Conchita dear. Hand me the towel, will you?"

Cay drew back from her listening post, seething. She tiptoed hurriedly out of the bathroom.

She stopped short in the center of the bedroom. She was no longer alone in these quarters. In the dimming twilight stood a tall elderly man, gazing at her, a casual bouquet of tropical blossoms clasped in his hand.

"Dear me!" he murmured. Then he seemed to smile. He slowly extended his arm, offering her the bouquet.

Chapter Eleven

Wednesday, December 5, 6:00 P.M.

Cay groped with her left hand through her swathing towel and accepted the bouquet, a cluster of crimson fleshy blossoms she didn't recognize. Her right hand was doubly busy, holding her improvised garb in place and thumbing open her purse catch so that the revolver would be accessible. She spoke softly, stepping back meanwhile to close the bathroom door; she didn't want to be heard by the Swans. "Thank you for your gallantry. I'm Cay Morgan—and you don't know how embarrassed. I suddenly realize this isn't the right room at all."

The tall man chuckled gustily. "I'm sorry you reached that conclusion." His voice was clipped and stagy British. "Forgive the familiarity under the circumstances. I'm Leonard Trefethen. Would a bit of light be considered ungallant?"

He tugged the light pull even as Cay was saying, "Not at all. A prowler must expect to stand inspection." She buried her nose in the flowers—which happened to have no scent whatsoever—and eyed him distrustfully.

His inspecting gaze was more roguish than suspicious. "Dear me!" he said. For a long moment his gray eyes, one brow cocked humorously, rested on her pale bare feet. His full-lipped mouth and bushy salt-and-pepper mustache curved in a broader smile. "Dear *you*, I should've said." His eyes traveled caressingly upward over the draped toweling, paused at the soft column of her throat and finally looked deep into Cay's calculating eyes. "I approve," said Trefethen with mock reverence. "How definitely I approve! Let's drink to these last few seconds, Cay Morgan."

"Drink to your imagination, you mean. No—I really mustn't." She decided he represented no immediate danger. "What I must do is explain that I thought this was Concha's room. I'm an old friend of her husband's, staying for dinner. I was showering when I set out to borrow a—well, something quite personal—from her."

As she lowered her lashes, Trefethen blew out his breath. He smoothed back his carefully groomed mane of iron-gray hair with a tanned and manicured hand. His tall thin body, a studied slouch of indolence about the shoulders, was clad in white ducks and an open-weave white shirt. He gave such a complete impression of being the ideal British colonial that Cay found him hard to swallow. She strongly doubted that he was even British. "Then," he said, "I'd need nerves of steel to question you further. Your case is reluctantly dismissed, damn it."

"Suspended," proposed Cay. "We'll have that drink later. Provided you're staying."

His eyes courted her towel-wrapped body again. "Lady fair, I am at your disposal forevermore. I have canceled all my plans for leaving Mazatlán tomorrow. The business world loses me, and you gain a slave."

"Business world?" She laughed. "And here I

thought I was being compromised with England's leading diplomat."

"Does the accent still show?" Trefethen asked fatuously. "No, despite my nineteenth-century leanings, I've enlisted in that twentieth-century crusade, the quest for the holy buck." He grimaced. "My line is soap. I'm a prospector, so to speak, for one of your American companies, Hutchins and Campbell. I round up the coconut oil that makes the soap that makes your skin so lovely."

"Then I may be grateful to you personally, I take it."

"I'd appreciate it, my dear. After all, I am a mainstay of the American way of life. Without me, there'd be no Cathay Soap. Without Cathay Soap, millions of women would reek, millions of men would be repelled, and the cradle of civilization—the amatory couch—would lie vacant." His mouth quirked with passing bitterness.

Cay saw Trefethen's plight—unless it was an elaborate pose. By appearance and inclination, he was born to play along the Riviera; instead he was forced to work for a living. But she still wasn't sure of his relationship to the Swans—especially to Concha, the unfaithful. Was Trefethen the lover? Cay asked innocently, "And does the Señora Swan smell better now that you've persuaded her to use Cathay Soap?"

"Good God, don't mistake me for a salesman of the filthy stuff! I merely contract for the oil. I was sent here to study the feasibility of building refinery equipment right here on the island, thus making less to do with the oil in the States, where labor's so much costlier. We're attempting the same thing all over the tropics." He broke off suddenly. "Oh, a dull, dull business."

"But I'm interested. And I'll still be later tonight, when I'm fully dressed."

"Will you really? Be interested, I mean? In that case, we can look forward to a simply wonderful night of it. I'll describe the processing of copra to you, step by bloody step." Again Trefethen gave his ironic chuckle. He patted her fingers, clasped round the crimson bouquet. "And whenever you bathe, think of me. Think of each bar of Cathay Soap as my hand, extended in greeting."

Cay smiled over her shoulder as she turned toward the hall door. "What a lascivious idea!"

"It was intended to be."

She made a face at him and, since he was watching from his doorway, turned toward the master bedroom. To substantiate her pretext for wandering, she borrowed from Concha a needle and white thread, inventing a torn hem. Then she returned to her own room, shed the huge towel, and completed her shower bath. She did her best not to think of the cake of soap as Trefethen's hand. Dressing herself carefully, Cay discarded the lace cape and left her shoulders bare. She let the bodice of the topless white drees settle to the point of minimum decency and then pinned one of the crimson blossoms between her half-revealed breasts.

Trefethen knocked on her door about seven-thirty. His eyes went immediately to the single dash of color in her costume, the provocative beacon she had fastened in the valley of her bosom. He said, "I'm now even more lost than you were earlier. Do you suppose you could guide a blinded man to dinner?"

With a sigh, she took his arm. "And I was expecting a protector," she said, trying to plant an idea in his head. "You disappointing men!"

"Protection? From your own aroused emotions, I hope? No, don't count on me there. I'm as dirty a dog as the next man."

"Splendid. I appoint you as my watchdog, in case a horde of murderous savages should come screaming out of the jungle. Isn't this a thrilling setting, though?"

She meant the front veranda, but she didn't really think so. A small table for four was set for dinner beneath a pair of orange lanterns. Beyond the oval of orange light, the shadows might conceal anything or anyone. The rustle she heard in the bushes alongside the veranda rail could be a lizard or a footstep. The night bordered too close upon their island of lantern light to allow her mind any rest. The gleam of beach and glint of black ocean seemed incredibly distant from the plantation house now that darkness had fallen.

She accepted an overly sweet cocktail from Spencer Swan. His eyes swam appreciatively behind his thick spectacles as he handed it to her. She drank it only because the others were drinking the same concoction. Keeping an eye on the mysterious reaches just beyond the veranda, Cay provided idle conversation for the two men attending her. Concha hadn't yet appeared. Trefethen paid Cay suave homage, commencing finally to appear annoyed at Swan's bumbling interruptions. Swan had the air of running madly to keep up with a dragging conversation.

Concha joined them on the second cocktail. Her greeting to Cay was a brief "Did you sew yourself up for the evening, Miss Morgan?" and thereafter she contributed little to the occasion. She had dressed her animal handsomeness effectively enough in a loose gold blouse and large-flowered peasant skirt, her feet in native sandals. However, she had not allowed for the contrast with her guest's white-sheathed blondeness, accented tonight by the subdued orange light. This transformed Concha into a heavy creature, coarse and lowborn. Her sensitive realization of the effect, added to the men's obvious concentration on Cay, tightened her mouth and destroyed her charm. "I think it is not too early to eat," she announced tensely.

Cay chose the chair with its back against the outer wall of the house so that nothing could happen behind her. Concha sat on her right. Trefethen was to her left and she faced Swan, whose gaze, both embarrassedly and defiantly, dropped constantly to the top of her dress. Concha glared at him openly.

"And the object of your life?" Trefethen asked Cay.

"To blow the world's biggest soap bubble." She was thinking about Hodd in Mazatlán, not knowing where she had gone. Perhaps she could secretly telephone the hotel after dinner. She began passing out hints about staying the night. Swan quickly took her up on it—and as quickly assured Trefethen that he would be returned to Mazatlán that evening as planned. It was Swan's first victory; he swallowed down one of his

nerve tablets with an unctuous smile. Cay wished
Trefethen were staying, and she wondered if Concha
felt the same way. But it still would be hours until
she'd be alone with the Swans, and if she could get the
husband off in a corner before that time… Yet so long
as she retained a grip on her purse, she had no real
fears for her safety. She ate warily.

"…we do, we mustn't miss the fiesta this week end,"
Trefethen was saying to her. "Mazatlán's patron saint is
the Virgin of the Immaculate Conception, for whom
our charming hostess is named." He directed a patron-
izing smile at Concha, then at once turned his attention back to Cay. "Concha is short for Concepción, you
know. And as I started to say, this Saturday is *el Día de
la Concepción Inmaculada.*"

"Last year I—" Swan began.

"The cathedral, of course, is the proper vantage
point," Trefethen interrupted smoothly. "Oh, were
you going to say something, Cay dear?"

"I have a friend who takes moving pictures. I wish
he could be there."

Swan looked startled. "Indeed? Who?"

Cay left it open. "My, I haven't seen him for years."

"You're not eating, Miss Morgan," Concha said
flatly.

Cay was taking no chances, although the food
looked delicious—fruit compote, turtle soup, and lob-
ster cocktails, followed by the entree of baked *pargo
colorado,* a red-fleshed fish. But she was avoiding anything served individually, helping herself only from
bowls in which the others participated. "I'm a bit
upset, señora. Perhaps the change of water…"

"Suppose I prepare something milder for you especially."

"Thank you, no. I'll just nibble here and there."

Concha bit her lip and shrugged and, a moment later, excused herself from the table. Her absence didn't affect the men's attentions. Cay wondered if they'd think it strange if she switched water goblets with Concha. The *pargo* was extremely salty but she didn't dare drink from her own glass. But her hostess returned too soon, resuming her chair without a word.

Trefethen was saying, "…nothing like Guadalupe Day at the Villa Madero, near Ciudad Mexico. Gad, there's a fiesta for you!"

Beneath the table, Cay felt an unseen hand touch her leg. She shot a quick accusing stare at Trefethen, but he was lost in his flow of reminiscence. "My luggage has been delayed and I didn't have…"

"Oh!" cried Cay sharply. With one cruel pinch, the hand had been removed. Her own fingers went to rub the spot. She wore no stockings on her tanned legs, and her fingers touched something warm and sticky. She brought her hand back to her lap, then glanced down at it. Her fingertips were red. Blood—blood from her leg, where someone, she knew with horrifying certainty, had just injected a hypodermic needle.

Trefethen had stopped talking and all three of them were looking at her curiously. Concha said coldly, "What now, Miss Morgan?"

Cay pushed back her chair. "Excuse me. I'm not feeling well." She was going to go to her room, lock herself in the bathroom, apply a tourniquet, have her gun ready… As she rose dizzily, she sensed the drug was already reaching up toward her brain. She must hurry...

Trefethen said, far away, "For God's sake, Cay, what is it?"

She recognized the wainscoting in the hall, her door with its knob eluding her grasp. She fell, heard herself gasp; she couldn't remember what had happened to her purse in the crushing spreading darkness. Time passed without meaning; dreams came and died... hands stripping off her clothes, a splash, then a whisper of the lonely sea. The darkness filled her being with the green taste of salt water...

Chapter Twelve

Thursday, December 6, 9:00 A.M.

A male voice, brusque and American, said, "Snap out of it, sister."

Cay opened her stinging eyes. Gradually a pillar of fire assumed the sharp outlines of a shaft of sunlight streaming down the narrow steps of a companionway. It brightened the dingy planking where it struck. She was in bed—in a bunk, rather—below the deck of some small boat. Above, through the open hatch, she could see a lovely square of blue sky, a wisp of cloud weaving back and forth behind a little mast.

"If you're going to heave," said the voice, "get in the head. Those are my only blankets."

"Who are you?" she croaked miserably.

"Walt. No, over here. Look over here. You're aboard my bucket, the Rainbow."

She turned her head, got him in focus. She gazed a long while. With great effort, her hand crept up to her mat of bangs. They were stiff with dried salt water but they seemed to have served their purpose in concealing her branded forehead. The rest of her long pale hair was a mess. She let her hand fall on the woolly blanket and whispered, "Walt. Rainbow. What a beautiful sight you are."

He was sitting on the bunk opposite her, his big hands gripped around a steaming mug of coffee, his elbows planted on the knees of his faded dungarees, his bare feet planted on the grimy decking of his boat. She hadn't expected to see a real live human being again. She pored almost greedily over the weather-beaten actuality of him, the muscled dark-tanned bareness of his torso with a streak of engine grease smeared down one heavy shoulder, the twin masculine slabs of his chest traversed by a bat-wing design of crisp black hair, occasionally wired with gray. His moody eyes were gray too, unfriendly scowl lines radiating from their corners to the gray bristles on his veined temples. But his cropped curly hair was mostly black, and she guessed he was about forty. His blunt sinewy face bore the intent savage stamp of a man who was trying to beat the world with his fists. To Cay, the sight of his brute solidity came as a dose of potent medicine. "I thought I was dead. What a beautiful sight…"

"You're getting delirious now," he said, unsmiling. She doubted that he laughed very often. "If you're through crying over yourself, see if you can keep down a cup of joe. Here—you can have the rest of mine."

Without rising, he handed the mug of coffee toward her and she saw that there might be another, more sensitive, side to him. On the little finger of his left hand he wore a cameo ring, the classic white profile of a Grecian girl, silhouetted against black and set in gold.

"Thank you." The hot mug felt good in her hands. His eyes had flickered as she reached for the coffee and she suddenly realized that she was completely nude under the tangle of brown army blankets. "Oh." She sipped at the bitter brew, frowning, trying to remember what had happened after she had risen from the Swans' dinner table. Her brain worked slowly, as if still drugged. "Excuse me—are my things drying out someplace?"

"No. When I fished you out of the water last night, you were naked as a jay bird. Except for your pearls."

"Oh." Investigating, she discovered she still wore her ear ornaments and her ring. "That's curious. Walt, tell me who you are, would you, please? And what we're doing wherever we are. I'm Cay Morgan, incidentally. Still a bit groggy."

"I'm a machinist when I feel like working and a fisherman when I don't. Satisfy you? The bucket's named Rainbow. No pedigree there, either. According to the sun, it's passing nine in the morning, Thursday, sixth December. Our position's some twenty miles south-southwest of Mazatlán, Mexico. This giving you a rough idea? Drink the coffee."

"Nine o'clock, Thursday." A full twelve hours since

she had passed out. "I was in the water when you found me?"

"About midnight. I was topside, doing a little trolling and a little drinking, when you came floating by. I hauled you in. After I squeezed some of the ocean out of you, you weren't so bad off, so I just stuck you in bed."

"And kept on going."

Walt stood up. He wasn't as tall as she had expected but there was plenty to him, well distributed. He said flatly, "I was having a fine time last night, just being alone on the ocean. You weren't so bad off as to need a whole damn hospital looking after you. You'll get back to civilization when the Rainbow and I feel like it, which'll be tonight. Any babe pie-eyed enough to take off her clothes and try swimming the Pacific has got to expect a little inconvenience."

"I can't take the time!" she burst out. "I have to get back!"

He looked down at her. "I've told you when. It beats swimming."

She was too weak to fight back the tears from her eyes. "I don't mean to carry on like this. I'm sorry if I've made you despise me. I don't have my life saved every night." She giggled, thinking, Oh, please, not hysteria. "I thank you, I can never thank you enough."

"You're welcome. Calm down."

"I'm trying to. I've been enough of a silly fool." But a lucky fool, she thanked her stars. She could understand the Swans' plan now, if not its motive. They had stripped her, ferried her out into the ocean, and dumped her overboard to drown. If she had ever washed ashore, the pearls would have proved her no victim of robbery. The police would have reached the same conclusion as Walt. "I'm afraid I was drinking last night too, past my limit. About eleven-thirty a moonlight swim seemed a splendid idea."

He grunted. "You were really crocked. There wasn't any moon last night."

Cay smiled meekly. "I try to lead a moonlit life."

"Sure." With a shrug, he said, "I vaguely remember some island off port about the time I fished you up. That where you want to go back to?"

"Oh, no," she said hastily. "After what happened— I'd look such an idiot, no clothes, having to explain where I was all night…"

"Won't your friends be worrying about you?"

"No, they're not the worrying kind." Not with her safely murdered. The idea caught; she thrilled to its implications. She was dead. The Swans had murdered her… *and the Trader would believe she was dead!*

Walt said, "How come the happy look all of a sudden?"

"Happy to be alive. Thank you again. You say we'll be getting into Mazatlán this evening? I won't be putting you out?"

"Hell, yes, you're putting me out. But you'll offer to pay me something and I'll shock you by accepting. I'm no hero." He turned abruptly toward the companion way, then hesitated. "If you're worried about last night, don't be. I didn't take advantage of the situation."

She watched him climb up out of sight. She grimaced drowsily; at least the notion had entered his head. She put the empty coffee mug aside, drew her knees up warmly against her body, and let her eyes close while she thought how much she'd like to take him down a peg or two. Not that she was ungrateful— and his aspect of strength, forthright to the point of cruelty, did appeal to her feminine nature—but the loss of a whole day in her timetable nearly made her ache. The steady engine noise, the shy lapping of waves on hull... all was peace, and she was trapped in it. She drifted off to sleep.

When she awoke, she was dripping with perspiration under the blankets. The sun had passed the meridian and the little cabin was a throbbing oven. She threw the blankets aside as soon as she saw that she was still alone. But the chug-chug of the engine beat a reassuring rhythm, a token that the man was nearby.

Her mind clearer now, she reviewed her situation. What had she lost in her brush with the Swans? Dress, shoes, underclothes—she had more. Wrist watch— regrettable, but... Loss of her purse was the major calamity. She still had most of her money at the hotel, and the tourist card could be dispensed with or possibly replaced. But how could she replace her precious revolver? She knew too well the impossibility of securing a gun in a foreign country. On the brink of doing battle with the Trader, she had been neatly disarmed. Cay ground her teeth.

Immediately the tiny below-decks quarters became too stifling for her. She climbed out of the bunk, reeled dizzily, and grabbed the wall to avoid collapsing. As her head cleared, she looked down at herself. Of course, Walt had seen her thus, clad in three pearls, but she had no intention of parading about that way. She began rummaging for something to cover herself. Lack of choice made her settle for the yellow oilskin slicker hanging on a nail.

When she put it on—it hung ungracefully below her knees—Cay's eyes widened to see what the slicker had concealed as it hung on the nail: a belt and holster. From the holster protruded the butt of a long-barreled revolver. She regarded it thoughtfully but restrained herself from touching it.

She emerged on deck, fluffing out her hair in the strong sunshine. The wheel spokes were lashed down with a belt and Walt sat on an upturned bucket by the stern, fishing with a heavy pole. He glanced back at her. "Things going better?"

"Much, thanks." She stood with bare feet braced against the gentle pitch and drank in the cool salt breeze. Off to port, Mexico was a purple shadow on the gleaming horizon. She gasped, "Hey, look at our wake! We're just going around in circles!"

Walt didn't turn to speak to her this time. "I'm trying for sailfish. I'll get you back this evening and that's—"

"Forget it," she snapped fretfully. The day was shot and there was nothing she could do about it. Only two days remained before the deadline Sunday, whatever the Trader planned to do then. After a gloomy look around at the boat, Cay found a clear space on the narrow deck and lay down in the sun with her head on a coil of rope. The rope was dirty but her hair needed washing anyway and it felt strangely satisfactory to be sloppy just once. She said, "First time I ever saw a blue Rainbow with a white stripe."

Walt only shrugged. So did she. She noticed that his stubby little bulldog of a boat was built very much like him. A far from new craft, it was pathetically shabby and nondescript compared to Swan's white cruiser.

She tried not to think about the time that was slipping out of her reach forever. With female calculation in her eye, she lay and watched the muscles play across his broad back. Perhaps he should be taught a lesson. What nice flesh he had; it would be so hard to the touch, yet resilient, and rough-smooth, and hot… The sweat glistened with his every move. What had he thought of her flesh last night? Those long spatulate fingers had held her, carried her, dried her. How tenderly? She had no way of knowing. Again she noticed the cameo ring and wondered if some girl had given it to him.

Walt caught some fish but small ones, Spanish mackerel and sea bass, not the big sailfish he was after. Later he smoked a pipe and the fragrance of the tobacco tantalized her. She called, "Don't happen to have a cigarette, do you?"

He looked around, surprised, as if he had forgotten her. "No. Sorry." And this time he kept looking at her as Cay had planned he should. The slicker had proved too hot on the sun-swept deck, so she had quietly slipped out of it. Now, folded and tucked, it was artfully arranged as a yellow band from thigh to breast. Finally Walt said, "You're going to burn."

She smiled. "Not till I die."

He turned away from her slowly, reeled in his line,

and stowed the fishing gear away. Then he went to the wheel and changed the lashing. He came back and stood over her. "I've set the course for Mazatlán. I guess that's what you had in mind with this strip tease. Now, if you feel like eating—"

"I'm not hungry." She gazed up at him, then closed her eyes. "And I had nothing in mind. I'm simply relaxing, for once in my life." She opened her eyes, satisfied now with the electric tenseness between them.

Suddenly he sat down cross-legged beside her prone figure. "You thought about when we make port? Clothes, I mean."

She trailed her fingers across the slicker. "Well, I've too much pride to go ashore like this. Perhaps you could go first and buy me something; any sort of dress'll do, and some sandals. Oh, and I'll need a purse, a large one. Will you mind buying women's clothes, Walt?"

His jaw muscles bunched. "You're working hard on me, aren't you?"

"I don't understand. Why should I?" Her right hand lay like a flower on her breathing bosom.

"I wouldn't know." He looked at the pearl on her finger. "You're not married?"

"Funny question." She let her lidded gaze rise smokily up the muscular column of his body, move casually about his face, and then plunge deep into his eyes. "Funny answer, too. No. No strings, no rings. I'm free as one of your beloved fish in your beloved ocean."

He leaned forward. She tingled as his hands, hot

but gentle, closed over her bare shoulders. "Fish get caught," he said huskily as his blunt savage face filled the sky above her and then his mouth came down hard upon hers.

She smothered her laugh against his lips. But immediately her body arched with surprise in the rising satisfaction of his kiss. She forgot about humbling him and blindly captured his head between her hands. The gradual relinquishing of the embrace was so sweet and tender that she wanted to cry. She felt no sly feminine vengeance now, only sheer joy as he mumbled, "God, you're a beautiful thing," against her cheek.

"Nice," she whispered, petting his shoulder. "So nice, Walt. Walt…" She scarcely recognized her own foolish laugh. "What's your last name?"

"Kilmer. Walt Kilmer. A tramp with a boat."

"No—wanderer. I'm a wanderer too. It sounds much nicer than tramp—especially for a woman." Oddly, the very nearness of him brought the lonely mood upon her. "Whatever I had in mind, Walt, it wasn't this." She strained toward another kiss and it was every bit as good.

"I've seen a lot of wanderers, places I've gone. You're the most beautiful." He began running his fingers through her hair.

"No. Stop."

"Hurt you?"

She dreaded the thought of his uncovering her scar. "Please, only a fetish of mine. Having my hair touched gives me cold shivers. Walt, sit up." He did, and Cay, expertly retaining her covering of oilskin, maneuvered around so that she could lie back in his arms. She sighed, outlining his harsh mouth with her finger. "I understand about being alone. My parents were wealthy, always traveling," she romanced, "and I grew up in a world of tall people who never cared to talk to a child. Now they're gone, I've got the habit, and I'm more alone than ever. They left me enough money so—"

"I haven't got anything."

"Except a mouth that does things to me. We're pretending, anyway."

"I wouldn't call it that. Last night— You don't know what a hell of a time I had keeping my hands off you."

"You're not asking me to let that pass for love, are you? When we've no time to make it mean anything?" She nestled her head plaintively against his bare chest. "No, all we've time for is a little innocent pretense and then that's that. You owe me that much, Walt. You've stolen a whole day from me."

"I don't get what you want, Cay."

"Lies. I want to be held, I want to be told lies, I want everything sweetness and light, the way we kissed." She closed her eyes and lifted her face toward his. His arms clenched tight about her. "There, that way. Who cares if it won't last?"

"Maybe I do," he said curtly. "We'll make Mazatlán in three hours. Then we'll have time to—"

"No. Let's settle that now. No more time then or ever. We're playing the wanderers' game today, playing that we have everything we want instead of nothing." She gazed soberly into his stormy gray eyes and said, "There's a choice, of course. You have a choice, Walt. Perhaps it's too cruel a game for a man."

He was silent a long time as the Rainbow chugged northward over the sun-bright waters. At last he lowered his weathered face and his mouth brushed hers again with the tenderness she wanted. "I always take what I can get," he said quietly.

Chapter Thirteen

Thursday, December 6, 6:00 P.M.

Their taxi pulled up before the Hotel Freeman at sundown. The driver came around to the door but didn't open it since neither passenger made a move to get out. His fares were simply gazing at each other gravely, so he courteously turned his back.

Walt said finally, "All of a sudden you're different."

"Am I?" parried Cay. "Night's coming. Or perhaps it's these clothes. You're not used to me in clothes." He had bought her a modest Mexican house dress of cotton as yellow as the slicker she had worn aboard the Rainbow. The color was his affectionate little joke. The simple dress fitted nicely, better than the huaraches that now graced her feet. A large crackly purse of inexpensive straw lay in her lap. But the totally unnecessary, and loving, touch was the *rebozo* he had brought to her. The long stolelike *rebozos* were the *mazatleco* fashion of the moment. Walt's purchase was filmy sky-blue wool, matching her eyes perfectly. She wore its two-yard length cowled about her head

and draped around her shoulders so that the intri-
cately knotted fringe fell down across her breasts. She
loved every inch of it.

"No, not the clothes," he said. "You."

"All right—me," she replied more harshly than she
had intended. "Will you come up and kiss me good-
by?"

In the open concrete vault of the Freeman's unfinished lobby, several tourists sat in rocking chairs and
watched the sun go down. One of them rose as Cay
and Walt came up the steps, and she saw, with a shock
of surprise, that it was Leonard Trefethen. She
thought: Then *he*, at least, hasn't heard of my death.

"Cay!" Even his bushy mustache seemed to beam as
he grasped both her hands. "Can't tell you how
delighted I am. Waiting, hoping, like a bloody slave,
until lo, here at last—" He became aware of Walt over
her shoulder. "I beg your pardon."

"Walt Kilmer—Leonard Trefethen," she said per-
functorily. The pair of them, in contrast, summed up
her unnatural life. Trefethen, for all his subtlety and
charm, was as untrustworthy as a hawk—the kind of
man she knew by heart, even to the dashing way he
wore his sport jacket hung over his indolent shoulders
like a cape. A contrast in clothing; Walt had donned
clean dungarees and a denim shirt and sneakers to
escort her home. He moved up next to her posses-
sively, staring hard at Trefethen, his mere presence
charging the atmosphere with a brute force that made
Trefethen appear bloodless and effete, without depth
or dimension. Cay had sensed that there were murky
deeps to Walt's character, hidden places that she half

regretted she would have no time to explore. But she never doubted for an instant which world was hers. She smiled dangerously at Trefethen. "Leonard, I'm really quite amazed to see you."

"Why? I knew you'd tire of that foolish island, a woman of your energies. Your fainting fit gave me rather a start, but after what Swan told me the doctor said—"

"Oh, yes, the dear doctor. Dr. Gonzales, wasn't that it?"

"I can't be sure. I didn't meet the chap, you know. While Concha put you to bed, Swan sent the boat in for him, and I returned to Mazatlán that same trip. I was faithful by telephone, though, Cay dear. I was counting on you to recover out of sheer ennui. Women are seldom ill long in dull places, I've found."

"No, there was nothing halfhearted about my attack. But I made a surprising recovery."

"Swan told me you were improving rapidly, but I asked myself, In what way can an angel improve?" Trefethen squeezed her hand. "Dinner tonight, obviously."

A sidelong glance at Walt's stiff face. "Not tonight, thanks. You may try me later if you care."

"I care. Watch your doorstep for me from now on."

When the elevator doors had closed out Trefethen's cheery smile, Walt growled in her ear, "What's that old buzzard to you, mind telling me?"

"I don't mind, but I haven't decided yet."

"I wouldn't mind breaking his neck."

"It might bend. It wouldn't break."

They got her key at the office and silently climbed

the remaining flight of steps to Room 22. The first thing she did upon entering, while Walt stared around, was to light a cone of sandalwood in the incense burner. With the rise of the thin stream of scented smoke, the afternoon was officially over, as much in the past as her girlhood. She sought in her suitcase for the money cache.

Walt said, "Nice quarters. Lots of space."

"More than I need, really. I mean, after all, three beds." She folded two five-hundred-peso notes and slipped them into his hand. He didn't say anything, only regarded her steadily and after a moment stuck the bills in his shirt pocket without even looking at them.

She had expected any behavior but that. She said weakly, "You see, that'll pay for the gas for your extra journey back, and the clothes you had to buy me, and this wonderful blue *rebozo*…"

"I suppose it covers everything. Want a receipt?"

"Oh, Walt!"

The hall door opened and George Hodd strode in. He said, "Would you mind telling me where—" before he discovered Walt standing there. His eyes narrowed. "Hello, mister. Who are you?"

Walt turned to Cay. "Good question. What would you call me?"

She saw all over his face the image he was building of her. She snapped at Hodd, "What brought you here? Did you ever hear of knocking?"

Hodd looked at the two of them, a haggard dignity tightening his features. "Well, excuse me," he said quietly. "When you turned up missing for twenty-four hours, I assumed it was my business to worry about you. Apparently not."

"Take it easy," Walt said flatly. "She was in good hands."

Hodd eyed Walt up and down, then said to Cay, "I suppose he's right." There was no doubt as to what he meant, and the door closing behind him sounded like a shot.

Walt surveyed the three beds again, silently. "Maybe this room isn't so big, at that."

"Make your own judgments," she said, and coldly extended her hand. "Good-by, Walt. Thanks for the lift."

"You said something about kissing good-by."

"Very well." Then his face was upon hers under the cowl of the *rebozo* and his mouth wasn't so much a part of the past as she had hoped. He squeezed her so close she could barely breathe and, blinded, she felt her knees melting at the contact. Her hands wandered senselessly; one last embrace wouldn't suffice, or two… "Please, Walt, please go now, darling." She broke away from him and leaned against the chiffonier for support. She tried to smile. "I want to keep what you've been so kind as to give me, darling. We'll leave this afternoon where it is. Tonight at twelve we can both tear it off the calendar. I'll never forget. Good-by, darling." She gasped. "No, Walt!"

But he wasn't trying to seize her. He reached past her, onto the chiffonier, and picked up the straw purse he had bought her. From it he extracted his long-barreled .45 revolver and slid the weapon inside his shirt. She watched him, aghast.

He said, "You shouldn't steal. You've got no business with a gun."

She laughed in his face.

He said, "I know trouble when I see it. You've got all the symptoms. Let me settle it for you."

"Believe it or not, I can take care of myself."

"Look, you think I'm just going to walk out of here and never think about you again, never know what's happened to you? I heard that double talk in the lobby with that guy a minute ago."

"Don't look for hidden meanings, Walt. Nothing ever happens to me."

His gray probing gaze caused a tremor inside her. He said, "When I dragged you out last night, you weren't hiding anything then." One hand caught her arm, the other brushed up her bangs for an instant.

Cay jerked free, numb with anguish. He had discovered her scar! "Get out," she whispered. "That was cruel. You had no right."

"I'm trying to make a right for myself," he said doggedly. "I'm not going to say good-by with you in trouble. Get that through your head."

She tried to hate him because she wanted no ties binding her to anyone. She wanted to cry with exasperation. "I don't need help, I don't need anything. You'd never understand the kind of woman I am. Leave me alone."

His face clouded darkly. "Goddamn it, Cay, you can't say good-by to a woman the day you fall in love with her!"

"Get out!" she screeched at him, and her breath

caught in a sob as she turned her back. "This afternoon was a mistake. Now please get out before I show you how much worse I can be. Keep what little you've got already!"

He didn't answer. But after a while she heard him sigh, and the sound of the hall door closing between them.

Cay stood there rigidly. Every muscle vibrated as she imagined each step he was taking down the corridor, down the stairs, the barriers of concrete and steel and tile multiplying inexorably. Now he was so far away, now farther; he had reached the lobby, the sidewalk...

Suddenly, without willing it, she ran to the French doors and flung them open and leaned over the rail of the balcony. "Walt!" she called wildly. "Walt, I'll see you again!"

Her blurred eyes found him as he spun around in the center of the Paseo Olas Altas, looking up at her unbelievingly, then his grin broadening. "When?" he shouted. The loungers and shoeshine boys and couples on the promenade stared appreciatively.

"Saturday night?"

He nodded vigorously. "Six o'clock? At the Rainbow?"

"Yes," she choked. "Oh, yes." He cupped his ear, unable to hear her. She bobbed her head until her cowl fell back on her shoulders and then, seeing he understood, she escaped hurriedly back into the room. Wonderingly she pressed her fingers to the tremendous beat of her heart, and raised her hands to her cheeks and felt the red heat there. She stroked the fringe of the *rebozo* he had given her; the woolen strands pulsated with her breasts. She lit a cigarette and smoked it shakily.

Chapter Fourteen

Thursday, December 6, 7:00 P.M.

She was wandering dreamily about her room, touching her belongings for reassurance, when George Hodd returned. This time he knocked. Cay looked at what he carried and said, "For heaven's sake, George!"

He said, "A boy left them in front of your door about noon. I took them up to my room and put them in water."

She laid the dozen long-stemmed red roses carelessly on the chiffonier and read the card. *"Please keep what you have stolen—my heart,"* with the flourishing signature of Leonard Trefethen. A little gift package had been attached to the green tissue paper that sheathed the rose stems; it contained a cake of Cathay Soap.

She looked at Hodd. His eyes were inscrutable. He said, "I read the card and opened the package. Under the circumstances I thought I'd better."

Cay smiled wistfully. "Don't be angry with me, George. Purely by accident I've collected a couple of admirers."

"Angry about what?" He sighed and sat down, gazing at her uncomfortably. "You hired me to gather information, that's all. When my client is attacked, witnesses a murder, then disappears for a night and a day, I find it a little difficult to concentrate on the assignment. Do you understand? I don't like the way things are heading."

"Premonitions?" she asked, "I do wish you had a gun, George. I need one. Mine was stolen."

Hodd said slowly, "I think the last thing I'd ever do is willfully put a gun in your hands." Cay laughed. He didn't, and became quickly impersonal. "No, I'm sorry to report I haven't spotted Diki or Goggles."

"I found Goggles. He's a plantation owner named Spencer Swan." She told him about Swan and Concha and Leonard Trefethen, and how she had missed being murdered. Hodd listened intently, looking his most dubious, and she talked fast to forestall any objections from him. "So start prowling. Find out about all of them before we run out of time. The town must know something about them. Find out how long they've been here, any kind of gossip."

Hodd agreed to that much, even made a few suggestions before leaving her. Then her ravening hunger caught up with her; it had been twenty-four hours since she'd eaten. Changing to shoes that fitted, she hurried down to Olas Altas and into the nearest café. Strolling troubadours serenaded her while she gorged herself in the sunken patio.

Afterward, struck by an idea, Cay walked briskly downtown, paying no attention to the warm blandishments of the evening. She purchased a large lead fishing sinker and two woven leather wallets, and hurried back to the hotel.

In her room, she worked for nearly an hour. First she reduced the wallets to their original strips of leather and then, with the heavy lead sinker as the core, skillfully braided the leather together again. Her product no longer resembled the original wallets. Instead, she now possessed a small but effective blackjack.

From her suitcase she dug out a tan suede purse and experimented at fastening her pliable bludgeon to the zipper, loosely, so that a strong tug would free it. She had carefully chosen the leather by color and, under superficial examination, the blackjack looked like part of the purse.

Her wrist watch was gone; she had no idea what time it was. She showered next and washed her hair and creamed her face thoroughly, expecting Hodd to report back momentarily. When he did not appear she surrendered to her fatigue and went to bed. In the thick gray dawn light she was aroused from vague fragments of nightmare. She stumbled sleepily to the door to inquire who had knocked.

"I am the night manager, Señorita Morgan," said a young man's voice in Spanish. "Pardon, but a Señor George has this moment telephoned to you this message. He demands you do not avoid the view from the Pérgola del Vigía."

"Señor George? *Un momento*." Cay began to wake up. "That's curious. A request—would you kindly ascertain if Señor George Hodd is now in his room? Room Thirty-two. *Gracias*."

Frowning, she sauntered the length of her stuffy quarters, pulled aside the drapes, opened the French doors to the balcony, and breathed the warm dawn air.

Below, all was peaceful on Olas Altas. A burro cart laden with milk clattered by; the taxis and shoeshine youngsters and wandering belt peddlers were already standing hopeful guard in front of the hotel. Out on the placid breast of the Pacific still rested the massive black freighter that had become an accustomed part of Cay's horizon, a lonely-looking hulk unable to clear the bay channel. Its mooring lights shone dimly and from its mast drooped the red merchant flag of India.

The night manager knocked again. No, Señor Hodd was not presently in his room.

Cay turned her eyes to the south, to the verdant Cerro del Vigía, which climaxed the peninsula of Mazatlán. On its sea-defiant cliffs she had seen Eduardo Valdes die. And now Hodd—apparently not having returned to the hotel at all last night—claimed to have discovered something at the Pérgola del Vigía, overlooking the southern tip of the peninsula.

Provided that the message had actually come from Hodd. With no room telephones, only the single instrument at the hotel desk, such a trap would be easy to set.

But how else to find out? Cay laid out her clothes swiftly: a silk-linen frock that was turtle gray down to the skirt yoke and white the rest of the way, white kid pumps, and the suede purse with its deadly new zipper fob. The purse clashed with her ensemble, of course, but her one weapon had become more important than high fashion.

Buttoning her dress, smoothing the wide lapels over the curve of her bosom, she heard a murmuring stir on the boulevard below. She went to the balcony.

Coal-black horses, black plumes nodding on their heads, drew a carved but somber funeral coach. She could see the corpse plainly through the glass side of the hearse. There were black-velvet-clad attendants from another century, and the family walked alongside holding black ribands attached to the coach's crucifixed roof. Behind marched the friends of the dead.

Cay shuddered and turned away. Premonitions? she asked herself. She bound her sky-blue *rebozo* about her shoulders and walked slowly downstairs to the taxi stand, thinking black awed thoughts. Who is there to march behind my coach? Who is there to hire a coach for me? I belong to no one.

Chapter Fifteen

Friday, December 7, 6:00 A.M.

A gaunt taxi driver bore her around the foot of Cerro del Vigía to the tip of the peninsula. Here, a narrow mole of rock continued into the ocean, connecting the mainland with the precipitous island of the lighthouse, called El Faro. Its beacon still flashed through the gray dawn sky. Cay paid off the taxi and watched it disappear. Then she surveyed this face of Lookout Hill.

Nothing moved in earth or sky. The towering bluff was overgrown but for a few raw gashes of yellow earth studded with colored pebbles. Watchfully, for in the dim light she could not see far, she began to climb the broad concrete stairway.

Six flights of the banistered steps zigzagged up to the crest of the bluff, interspaced with square landings of checkerboard tiles. She scanned the steps and landings carefully for chewing-gum wrappers but saw no signs that George Hodd had ever come this way.

She reached the top, winded, and the surf below mumbled the only sounds. She was alone, terribly alone. The pergola was an oval observation platform of tile, encompassed by a low concrete wall. Enclosing one end stood a semicircular arcade of ten classic pillars supporting an open-beam roof. Backing this bucolic structure, a thin screen of pine trees whispered among themselves. The pines appeared to be the only feasible point of ambush, so Cay investigated them first but could see beyond them only the natural brushy movements of a hilltop waking to morning. A path wandered off across the hilltop. On a stone pedestal in the center of the pergola crouched an old coastal cannon, a relic of Mexico's colonial epoch.

There was nothing to see but the distant lighthouse and limitless hazy miles of ocean—yet there had been the message. She sat down at a marble table with benches and thoughtfully smoked a cigarette. Perhaps Hodd had meant he was making an appointment with her. As she waited, her concentration wandered. The marble furniture had been dedicated in *reparación* by a *mazatleco* doctor. For what fault, real or fancied? She dismally recounted her own list of sins. The day's first buzzard appeared, wheeling high over her head.

The sun rose in red grandeur, painting the pergola pink, turning the ocean from gray to dazzling blue. Now, far to the south where the mainland jutted, she could see a corner of Isla de Puesta del Sol, Swan's island. Could Hodd have seen… No, at night the island would be invisible.

She glanced up and saw that the original buzzard had been joined by another, and while she watched still more black wings came flapping in across the waters from the lighthouse. For a moment or two she admired their graceful flight, the effortless soaring as they glided around and around, descending gradually.

And then she sprang up, a sudden tremor chilling her stomach. For buzzards didn't gather over one spot without reason.

She ran to the wall and stared down the steep shoulder of the bluff, seeking the hub of the great birds' circling descent. What gray dawn had obscured she saw distinctly in the fresh sunlight. Nearly at the bottom of the cliff, embraced by the many fat green arms of a cactus, she saw the twisted trousered legs of a man. The rest of his body was hidden by undergrowth.

Scorning caution now, Cay raced down the interminable steps, two at a time. A buzzard had just settled beside the body, and at her vicious charge it lurched into the air again, squawking in surprise and distress. Cay threw a handful of dirt at it to hasten its flight. All the buzzards retreated to a safe distance in the sky as she knelt beside the man.

George Hodd was stiff with death. His neck was broken, his eyes wide with accusation. Somehow he had been lured to the pergola; he had been pushed or thrown over the edge.

"Oh, George," whispered Cay. With a pang, she

realized that she had sacrificed him to the Trader, to her obsessive ambition. "Oh, George, I'm sorry, I'm sorry…" She touched his cold hand gently with her fingertips. Her eyes burned with sorrow. "You disliked violence so," she said. "Why did I ever let you get mixed up with me? Here—close your eyes now."

She did that gently, thinking how typical it was of the Trader to play with her in this fashion. The only purpose of the false telephone message had been to fling Hodd's death in her face. She crouched by the twisted body, the frustrated hate trembling through her, and she made a fresh vow to George Hodd. "Nothing will ever stop me now…"

But she was no longer alone with him. An unnatural sound impinged itself upon her consciousness, stealthy footsteps creeping down the concrete stairway behind her. She didn't move; the footsteps ceased. She sensed that the unknown was standing directly in back of her, watching her.

Secretly moving her hand, she detached her plaited blackjack from the purse. Then, in one continuous blur of angry movement, she stood up, whirled, and threw overhand. The lead-weighted missile sang through the air like a bullet. The man on the stairs clapped his hands to his groin and bent double, gasping out a quick sharp cry of pain.

In a catlike pounce, Cay vaulted over the concrete banister onto the steps. She struck out with fury, a knuckled judo cut that kept the man from straightening until she had caught his throat in the crook of her elbow. Vengefully, she forced him backward over her hip, trapping him in a spine-breaking, neck-strangling hold.

Despite his bulging eyes and purpling face, Rómulo María Felix did his best to smile gallantly at her.

Chapter Sixteen

Friday, December 7, 7:00 A.M.

She whispered, "Why did you have to kill George?"

Behind their dark glasses, Felix' eyes distended helplessly. Cay gave his neck a cruel twist and suddenly dropped his plump red-shirted form on the steps. Snatching up her blackjack, she stood over him while he fought for breath and wiped his eyes with his jeweled fingers. "Tell me the truth," she warned softly.

"*Caray!*" he gasped. "You jest. My neck is broken and you jest."

"You're wrong twice. Tell me the truth before I make you half right."

"I've only followed you," said Felix, smiling feebly up at her. "That is certainly all. What's the crime in following a great beauty—even if she is the most dangerous woman in the world?" He added mournfully, "Ah, *huera*, how fierce you are!" as he massaged his neck.

"I don't like to be called that."

"But you won't kill me so long as I keep talking, will you, *huera*? See, I have been investigating your itinerary ever since Monday morning. Not personally, of course, but through the co-operation of certain local drivers. I myself have been recuperating from our first meeting." He touched the healing scar on his cheek left by Cay's gun. "I've decided that it adds a certain raffish handsomeness, as of a duel." A racking cough interrupted him; he clutched his throat. "*Espíritu santo!* You've incapacitated me again."

Cay raised the blackjack and said between her teeth, "I shall count to three quickly."

"I've never killed anyone, believe me! I mourn for you and your lost friend. Oh, yes. My original interest in you was routine curiosity. Now with this morning's tragedy—but particularly since your visit to the island—I feel that an alliance is indicated. We should pool our strength toward our common objective."

"Alliance," repeated Cay grimly. She slowly lowered the blackjack. She climbed over the banister again to recover her purse from beside Hodd's body. Since Felix made no move to flee during her absence, she was inclined to believe him. "Alliance?" she said, returning to the steps.

"Not only with myself," he assured her. "A third party is anxious to encounter you." His stout little body labored to its feet. "Now I doubt if you can resist accompanying me." He grinned knowingly.

She didn't reply but simply followed behind him as he climbed the steps to the pergola. They followed the path across the hilltop to the place where a taxi waited.

Cay couldn't look back as they rolled down the slope toward the city. She didn't care to see the buzzards circling lower now that George Hodd was left alone again. She herself could not afford the delay of reporting a murder, but she prayed that he would be found quickly.

Mazatlán bustled with morning shoppers and schoolbound children as their taxi honked its way across town, guided through the maze of one-way streets by red-lettered *"Circulatión"* arrows pasted on building corners. Felix chattered; Cay brooded; the driver piloted them northward into a comfortable suburb along the Avenida Rouiles Serdan.

"We've arrived," said Felix. The block of houses, as usual in the city, presented a low common façade of thick brown masonry, the dwellings differing only in the grille pattern of the windows or the color of the door opening directly onto the sidewalk. Felix dismissed the taxi and then used a key on a green door numbered 477.

The door opened into a short cool passageway of scrubbed black tiles; one of Mazatlán's ten thousand bicycles leaned against its stucco wall. The passage led in standard fashion to a spacious hot-country living room, which bordered without intervening wall on the inevitable patio. The verdant roofless square of patio was the core of home life; the house girded its tropical luxuriance like a massive square flower pot.

To prevent chance glimpses from the street, a thin lattice screen had been placed at the end of the corridor. Although Cay still stood in the entrance passage, she could see that a burly man was sitting at a small spidery table in the living room. Sunlight from the patio limned his monstrous silhouette sharply against the lattice screen. His head, a blob of shadow, turned gradually toward the people he had heard enter his house.

Felix called to the shadow, "It's I, Rómulo María

Felix. Don't fear." And to Cay: "Always a man must be careful, even with his friends. Right?"

She rounded the screen and entered the tiled living room, a gloomy bower when compared to the greenly brilliant patio just beyond. Most of the furniture stood on legs of filigreed iron; a velvet wall tapestry needed cleaning badly. The flesh-and-blood counterpart of the shadow was pointing a nine-millimeter Lahti pistol in her direction, a Swedish automatic nearly ten inches long. She said calmly to Felix, "This represents anxiety to meet me, eh?"

"Precautions, precautions," Felix shrugged. He made a slight bow to their host. "I have here the Morgan woman, D'Hureau. Her partner, the George Hodd, has been sadly killed." Cay couldn't be certain that he wasn't winking behind her back.

D'Hureau's fleshy freckled face told her nothing. His lids drooped a little over his chilly eyes and, hooded, they regarded her like two tiny cobras. Cay gazed back as impassively, surveying this unknown quantity from his dankly curly mop of red hair to his sandaled feet. His toenails needed trimming. D'Hureau's grossly powerful body sat in a wing chair that seemed too small for him. He wore yellow-flowered pajama trousers and a soiled undershirt. The profuse red freckles ceased at his white womanly throat but began again on his shoulders, increasing in number as they descended his thick arms, until his forearms were almost a uniform fiery red. The freckling disappeared abruptly at his wrists, for his strangely dainty hands were covered by gloves of white silk. When he spoke at last his voice was husky

and guttural. He said scornfully to the Mexican,
"Through pity did you bring her here?"

"I don't allow pity," Cay interposed. "I forced your
Felix to bring me here. I've a hunch our goals are the
same."

Felix gave her a sharp look. "No, D'Hureau, it was an
idea that presented itself to *me*. She may be able to—"

"I did not engage you for your ideas," said
D'Hureau.

Cay looked at the automatic casually threatening
her middle. "You might be mannerly enough to put
down that scrap iron. As you can see, I'm harmless."
Felix laughed. Cay smiled lazily and added, "At least,
I'm not at all dangerous to my friends."

"Oh, none of us can ever be friends," said D'Hureau.
But he laid the Lahti pistol on the wood mosaic of the
little table before him and his gloved hands picked up
the other object there, a misshapen black lump resem-
bling coal. He fondled it pensively. "Why should I waste
my time with you? Tell me reasons."

"Logistics." She kicked an ottoman closer to the
parquet table and sat down, crossing her legs deliberately. D'Hureau didn't even glance at her legs. "Three
is a larger force than two."

"You seem quite certain that I need force."

"Won't you, when the Trader finds out you're
here?"

Felix, leaning against the wall, chuckled in an
I-told-you-so tone. D'Hureau blazed at him suddenly, "Quiet, you little fat fool!" Then he mused
gloomily over Cay's upturned attentive face. "So you

wish to work for me. I see. How steep is your price?"

"You're wrong. I don't want to work for anyone except myself. However, we may be able to trade my brains for your muscle at the crucial time." She remembered what Felix had said earlier. "You see, I've been to the island."

"Yes, you have," breathed D'Hureau, sticking out his lower lip at her. Then he toyed with the black lump in his hands, studying it. "I have brains of my own— but an introduction to the island might amount to something. How much do you know?"

A difficult question. D'Hureau obviously knew something about the Trader's present activities. Yes, an alliance with her host would serve her own deadly purpose well. Cay grinned shrewdly. "I've come to Mazatlán, haven't I? I know it's big business to bring the Trader here. I trust you can supply any details I may have overlooked."

D'Hureau didn't bite on that. "And your share? Not too steep, now."

"There are only two of us. A straight split." She heard Felix cough insinuatingly. "You can pay Señor Felix out of your half."

"You are vastly ridiculous, as are all women." D'Hureau yawned. Immediately he was smoldering again, shouting at her, "I'm not interested in you at all! What strumpet is worth such a price?"

Cay jumped to her feet. She said steadily, "Say what you like after I'm gone, but don't ever dare to call me names again. Good-by, you two. I'll be rich while you're still rotting here."

"No, no," exclaimed Felix. "Don't let's disagree! Don't let her go, D'Hureau! She is the help we can use. Otherwise, the treasure—"

"She's not going," said D'Hureau. "Look at her, merely bluffing. A team of elephants couldn't drag her away from us. I'll mention again the word 'treasure.' Ha, see her eyes light up! No, she won't be leaving us."

"I accept your apology," said Cay with a small frosty smile. She reseated herself. "Very well—a third share, then. Done."

"Done too greedily, little lady. We'll agree on a fifth."

"No, we won't. I tell you I won't do with less than a third."

"What a ridiculous woman! Listen to me. A fifth of *something* is worth considerably more than a third of *nothing*. Particularly when I would estimate your share at close to a million dollars!" His eyes never left her face. "Yes, a *million*, Miss Morgan. That's what I said."

She couldn't help blinking. She could feel the tingling perspiration break out on her palms. She said, "I've tried to spend promises before."

D'Hureau didn't speak. He signaled to Felix, who brought from behind the divan a physician's black bag, old and scratched. In places mildew had stained the cracked leather. D'Hureau opened the bag and took out a narrow-bladed scalpel. Then he picked up his coallike lump and with the scalpel point delicately shaved away a thread of the black color. "See for yourself," he said, handing it to her.

The lump was heavy in Cay's hand. She got her lorgnette from her purse and carefully examined the line D'Hureau had etched in the black. The line was a mellow golden color. Felix crowded her shoulder to look also and his tongue clucked rapturously.

"You are looking at pure gold," said D'Hureau, a little unnecessarily. "The dark coating is from burial in the earth for a long time. This sample alone is worth over a thousand dollars, and it is merely part of an ingot. The Trader's business in Mazatlán involves many, many ingots. Do you wish a fifth share in it or don't you?"

Cay coolly returned the chunk of precious metal and took her time putting her lorgnette away. No wonder the Trader had cautioned Valdes not to underestimate the size of the coup! At this exhilarating moment, the allure of gold intensified all her thoughts of vengeance, and her long search became not only a vendetta, but a road leading her to fortune. Once the Trader was removed... then she would see how the gold should be divided and between whom. She said, low-voiced, "I agree to a fifth share."

"You're thinking that you will play along with this old fool," said D'Hureau amiably. "You'll co-operate until the vital moment, and then..." He snapped his, gloved fingers softly in Cay's face. "Like that, of course." Without warning he shouted at her, "Well, don't attempt it! I'll crush you without compunction if you act to trick me, understand?"

"It works both ways, D'Hureau." Cay met his eyes gravely. "So let's not make so much noise about it, shall we?"

"Yes, we'll get on together." He lapsed into morose silence, staring at nothing. Cay waited, watching the shadows of banana leaves move on the tiles and listening to the buzz of insects busy among the exotic flowers. Finally, D'Hureau stirred his big hulk. "Consider. Do you know the Trader yourself?"

"Only enough to want to kill him."

"Indeed. For my part, mere death would hardly repay me." D'Hureau flexed his silk-clad hands ominously. "I was, you understand, once his employee."

Cay held her breath. "Did you— Then you know him on sight?"

"We have never met. On rare occasions I've spoken to him, yes, but only by telephone. We conversed in French, which I don't believe is his native tongue, since it happens to be mine. I'm from Equatorial Africa, Miss Morgan, not France. My father was an expatriate, my mother was Irish. My parents devoted a great waste of money to my education as a physician. I lacked the necessary unimagination to be a penniless outlander medico. After my troubles with the authorities, I turned to more lucrative pursuits as a prospector and, above all, an expert on gems and precious ores. I tell you this to demonstrate the extent of my experience in these matters. In the Bultfontein fields I was drawn into the Trader's orbit. Soon afterward he sent me to Panama."

Cay shrugged. "I prefer to discuss Mazatlán, D'Hureau."

"But it was in Panama that I saw this gold sample for the first time. A man named Meeuwenberg brought it to me for an evaluation, a basis of negotiations with the Trader. He was a creature whose tongue could be readily uprooted by wine, and so I learned the story. Meeuwenberg was merely acting as agent for an American, Spencer Swan."

"Swan? I didn't know the meek were intended to be *that* blessed."

"It does seem unfair. But this Mexican state of Sinaloa is one of the richest mineral areas in the world. Only the federal government's opposition to foreign capital has retarded its progress. Yet, during the Spanish rule, billions were dug out of the ground here and carried home to Europe. The ingots were embossed with the stamp of Arispe, meaning they were destined for the royal treasury."

"But the Spaniards were driven out a hundred years ago."

"Longer. But what does time matter to pure smelted gold?" D'Hureau rolled the blackened lump over with his forefinger. "See, the stamp of Arispe. You wonder whence it came. At the time of the revolt in 1821, a Spanish ship was harbored here in Mazatlán, undergoing repairs and loading ingots from El Tago mine in the mountains. The Spaniards assumed that the Iturbide revolt, like the Hidalgo rebellion eleven years earlier, would be put down. Yet, fearing capture of the gold cargo, they removed it to the Isla de Puesta del Sol nearby and buried it there. However, the revolt was not put down. It succeeded and the Spaniards could never return for their gold."

"And Swan had the luck to find it," Cay said. "But why his secrecy?"

"The Mexican government. If they knew of the cached bullion, they'd probably confiscate it, as they have done in previous cases of rediscovered hoards.

The foreigner Swan can't own property—the island is in his wife's name. Consequently, when he stumbled onto the ingots, he merely carved off his embossed sample and covered the burial pit over again. He did make soundings, to determine the area and depth of the find. Meeuwenberg's estimate was seven tons! Suppose, on a round basis of eight hundred thousand dollars per short ton..." D'Hureau's lips worked with excitement. "Such a find will take time to disinter, of course. It raises transportation problems. But that lies in the future. What Swan did was to send Meeuwenberg to find an undercover marketer, such as the Trader."

"Where's this Meeuwenberg now?"

"He died," said D'Hureau simply. "But not, unfortunately, before his tongue wagged further. A certain hound in whom I reposed my personal plans betrayed me to the Trader. I was captured and the Trader demanded this sample of the gold. I substituted a nicely plated rock in its stead and, since the deception wasn't immediately discovered, I was allowed to live on. Ah, the kindly Trader does not care to kill—not when there are other punishments."

The repressed savagery in his husky voice made Cay shiver. She passed it off as another shrug. "I won't intrude in your private affairs."

"Why shouldn't you know? You've been staring openly at my gloves! Why shouldn't you see?" Furiously, D'Hureau tore the white silk from his right hand, then thrust the hand under Cay's nose. "See how the Trader wished me to live and remember, not die and forget!"

Branded across the soft flesh of his palm was the puckered red shape of a T.

Chapter Seventeen

Friday, December 7, 9:00 A.M.

Felix sucked in his breath. *"Mama mía!"* The little divorce detective was more affected by the brand than he had been at the sight of Hodd's body; for him living disfigurement was plainly more formidable than sudden death. His hand strayed up to his healing cheek.

Cay said nothing, her face an implacable mask. She looked at the hideous scar, remembering the days of near insanity when her own brand was as fresh and glaring red. The silk whispered as D'Hureau replaced his glove. He asked quietly in French, "You understand now why his death cannot satisfy my appetite? Die he will, yes, but only after I've dissected him."

Cay said, "As you say—provided you find him before I do, doctor mine."

Felix laughed nervously. "I think we companions should converse in English or Spanish, please. Are you discussing me?"

She switched back to English, still addressing D'Hureau. "My claim to the Trader was staked long before yours. Someone cheated me out of Valdes, but— What's that?" Cay stood up hurriedly as a thin musical chiming sounded in the room. She had heard its faint fairy tune once before, from the shadowed *glorieta* where Eduardo Valdes had died. She reached for the long pistol but D'Hureau's hand was pressed firmly over it.

"I think not," he said, scowling.

"That noise! Aren't we alone in this house?"

The chiming had ceased. D'Hureau turned back the cuff of his left glove and indicated his wrist watch. Its hands pointed to nine o'clock. "Where are your nerves, woman? That was merely my wrist watch striking the hour."

She sat down on the ottoman slowly. "Then you knifed Valdes."

"Scalpeled might be the accurate verb. Do you object?"

"Rather useless, now." Cay bit her lip. The chime of the wrist watch at sundown that evening, the neat surgical thrust directly into Valdes' heart... all D'Hureau's doing. "Then you were the person on the bicycle who passed my *araña*."

"I suppose so. Because I am known to the Trader's organization, I seldom stir from this house I've rented. But that day Felix—whom I employ as eyes, ears, and legs—was on other missions. I followed Valdes personally."

"You should have stayed home. Killing Valdes was a stupid trick. He knew the Trader personally."

D'Hureau sullenly rubbed his hand over his red curls. "Don't offend me. I admit the blunder. Yet—I spoke of a hound who betrayed me. A skull-faced hound, a vile oily Spaniard of a hound, Valdes. When I saw the glorious opportunity for retribution... Well, remember that my temper sometimes overrides my best interests, Miss Morgan."

"I'll listen carefully for your music." She smiled affably.

"I won't make that error again. My watch let slip my presence to Valdes. I had turned off the hour strike, but the bicycle ride evidently jolted it on again. Depend on my not wearing it, should I ever choose to creep up behind you."

Felix flashed a cheerful grin. "Are we allies here or are we not? If we are, let's have an end to these veiled threats, which don't seem to me very veiled at all. Why can't we trust one another as little children?"

Cay nodded. "You're right, Felix. Considering what happened to Mr. Hodd, I'd say we'd damn well better pull together. None of us is exactly safe. You, D'Hureau, have deprived the Trader of his chargé d'affaires. My slight efforts have consisted of trying to enrage him with his own signature. I agree that the Trader seems to regard murder as a last resort—but the death of George Hodd rather proves that our opponent is getting pretty exasperated with our imminent interference. Granted, we three may lack mutual respect, but we'd better cooperate simply out of fear for our"—a glance at D'Hureau's gloves—"skins."

"Well spoken, *huera,*" said Felix, patting her shoulder. "As a mark of trust I'll tell you where D'Hureau hides his lump of gold. In the patio, in the platano tree yonder."

"Trust? Trust?" roared D'Hureau. "With you two thieves already plotting to steal from me?"

"I don't steal," said Felix blandly. "Believe what you

please of our beautiful guest—she may be a thief or worse, come to think of it—but I've never stolen a centavo in my life. I mentioned the matter only to avoid future confusion, in case of your death."

D'Hureau subsided but he was not amused. Cay chuckled, and carefully marked the location of the banana-like platano tree.

Guardedly, they exchanged information. D'Hureau, while en route to Mazatlán, had hired Rómulo María Felix in Mexico City. Aside from his vicious foray against Eduardo Valdes, the big ex-doctor had done little but wait for the Trader to expose himself somehow. Felix's great contribution had been to discover Cay's presence, an involvement that had puzzled both men considerably. D'Hureau, although acquainted with Jack Diki, hadn't even learned that the slant-eyed assassin was in Mazatlán. He did contribute various minor details about the Swans. Cay was surprised to find out that Spencer Swan had bought the island only two years before; prior to that his background was unknown. Cay had automatically assumed that the Swans were native *mazatlecos*, or nearly.

"And you think that the Trader is bargaining with the Swans directly?"

"I'm certain of it," said D'Hureau. "He has his wise passion for anonymity, true, but in this case, whom could he trust completely?"

"*Verdad*," agreed Felix with a sly smile. "You taught him a lesson in that regard."

Cay described Leonard Trefethen and told what she knew about him. As D'Hureau had never heard of any such person in the Trader's organization, they were again stalemated. Since Swan did operate a copra plantation, it appeared only too possible that Trefethen was no more than the coco-oil contractor he claimed to be.

D'Hureau chewed the insides of his freckled cheeks. "We must act, *act*," he stated. "Before Sunday, needless to say. While we weigh the intentions of every stranger in Mexico, our ingots are likely to be stolen from us. We must find a way to the Trader. Then we'll be free to deal with the Swans."

"Why do you two laugh at my plan?" asked Felix. "You say there is no mystery about this Diki, except where he may be keeping himself. At least we know Diki when he is before our eyes. Let us seize him."

"No," said D'Hureau. "What little he may know, he wouldn't tell us."

"Don't be too sure. I have certain foul talents that I've always longed to express." Felix sighed. "With heated pliers, with needles in the ears—"

"No! I tell you some kinds of men cannot be induced to talk. Torture without death in store is useless. Diki would force us to waste our time while we slowly killed him. He's insensible, else he wouldn't be what he is."

Devoid of practical ideas, all of them lapsed into grumpy individual silences. After a while D'Hureau shambled into the kitchen and prepared a highly spiced midday meal. He was an excellent chef. Cay's compliments pleased him and, over coffee, she put on her brightest manner and tried charming him out of his awkward but invaluable pistol. But the Lahti automatic could not be wheedled, borrowed, or purchased

from D'Hureau, and he made her cross by at last bel-
lowing at her to shut up. He stuck the gun in the waistband of his pajama trousers and sank into the wing
chair for his siesta; the heat of the day was upon them.
Felix napped upon the divan but Cay stalked into the
patio. She took a perverse pleasure in exposing herself
to the baking sun as she paced around the dirt paths
and thought vigorously. Presently she realized that
neither of her companions were sleeping; they were
watching her through half-closed eyes.

She rejoined them in the cool living room. "Perhaps
the quickest way to the Trader is through the gold,"
she suggested. "Perhaps we should consider the gold
our first problem, for the time being."

"How do you mean?" asked D'Hureau.

"If we could secure the gold, we'd have the Trader
on our necks soon enough. I've been thinking about
Spencer Swan. He knows where the gold is. For that
matter, we've decided that he knows the Trader on
sight. Be that as it may, we've got to tackle somebody,
and Swan would seem the easiest choice."

"Very good. A weak link, yes," ruminated
D'Hureau. "By this approach, the affair simplifies.
We'll put your womanly wiles to the test. You return to
the island and—"

"That won't do," Cay interrupted. "I can't return to
the island. I won't risk it. I'm not wanted there." She
explained about the attempt on her life.

D'Hureau glared at her. "You tart! So you have no
entree to the island after all!" He shook a furious
finger in her face. "By trickery you made me believe
you had value to me! But you are worthless!"

"My value is that I'm smarter than the pigs I associate with," Cay said icily. "Do you want to hear my plan?"

"No! Not if you can't go to the island!"

"I think I can make the island come to me. At least, the part of the island we want—Swan."

D'Hureau grunted. When he spoke again, his temper had waned to mere sarcasm. "You will blow kisses toward him, perhaps?"

"Why be that subtle about it? Swan knows what I'm after, and I know where his interest in me lies. I'm not sure how much desire I can arouse over twenty miles of telephone line, but..." Cay paused, then snapped her fingers. "The telephone! That's one answer. Suppose the telephone cable to the island should be cut. Wouldn't that bring Swan to town to arrange a repair job? Felix could do the cutting."

"I?" exclaimed Felix. "I'm no deep-sea diver."

"Cut it in shallow water where it comes ashore. You can at least swim, can't you? Once Swan is in Mazatlán, I'm certain I can catch his eye. How much I can get out of him remains to be seen."

"We want him to talk to all of us," D'Hureau reminded her heavily. "Not just to you."

"Of course, he won't notice you two hiding under the bed. Is that how I'm supposed to win his favor? 'Spencer dear, pardon me while I blindfold you. No, we're quite alone, my sweet, those are rats you hear.' Bah!"

D'Hureau clapped his hands. "Wait! We *shall* blindfold him. We shall blindfold his will power." He picked up his medical bag from the floor and dug out a small grimy bottle. Cay read the penciled label and looked doubtful. D'Hureau said, "He can be reduced to a mere answering machine. He'll be unable to resist us. All that is necessary is that he drink with you."

"Well, Spencer Swan is no fool. He's not going to swallow a mickey simply because it's been warmed between my pretty hands."

"I have a suggestion," said Felix, and they wrangled over the plan for the rest of the afternoon. Gradually a feasible scheme evolved. Its only major flaw, to Cay's mind, was that the project left the time of operation to chance and Spencer Swan. She fiddled with the fringe of her *rebozo* uneasily. Tomorrow night she was supposed to see Walt Kilmer again at his boat. But, she rationalized, perhaps she would be finished with Swan by then. Certainly she would be.

As D'Hureau's wrist-watch chime counted out the sundown hour of six, he brought out an unopened bottle of Rhenish wine and poured glasses for the three of them. "As a man of the tropics I never allow myself to drink until sundown," he told Cay in a manner almost amounting to good humor. "And as a connoisseur I never allow uncorked wine to stand over. Hence, a fresh bottle every evening."

Cay held up her glass. "To Lady Luck," she said.

"You take too much upon your sex," reproved D'Hureau. "Luck is more probably a gentleman."

"Neither," put in Felix. "An animal, I'd say. In this case, likely a jackal."

"Then we drink to ourselves," said Cay. In the dimming room, they glanced at one another and drank, unsmiling.

Chapter Eighteen

Saturday, December 8, 5:00 P.M.

Cay leaned out the window of her parked taxi and said, "Hello, Spencer." He stopped short on the sunny steps of the telephone company building, mouth and eyes agape. His white sport shirt and yachting cap already looked a little wilted and he seemed to shrink inside them.

She said, "I thought you'd never come out. I'm so tired of waiting."

"Waiting?" His pointed features twitched as he slowly came over to the side of the taxi. He looked up and down the teeming street. "What are you doing here? Difficult to think this is a coincidence."

"No, I've been waiting all afternoon to talk to you." Swan licked his lips, preparatory to turning away, and Cay went on, hurriedly, "Surely you can spare me a few minutes of your time after all the trouble I've gone to—cutting your phone cable."

"You—" He took off his spectacles and wiped them nervously and put them on again. "Cay, I'm afraid I have to rush over to—"

Her hand slid through the taxi window like a friendly serpent. "Don't be upset with me," she said, touching his arm gently. "I don't bear a grudge, Spencer, if that's what's bothering you. Business is all I have on my mind, despite what may be preying on yours." She opened the car door invitingly so that he could get a good full view of her. "And I assumed—after the time we were together on your cruiser—that you wouldn't object to seeing me again. Was I wrong about you?"

His circumspect appraisal of her, through lonely eyes, told her she wasn't. Counting on her femininity as the opiate to dull his initial sense of danger, she had dressed with careful simplicity for the encounter. Her hair was brushed to the pearliest sheen possible. High heels and clinging nylons accented the curve of her calves. Her skirt, of finely black-checked silk, lay across her thighs in box pleats. Through her filmy white blouse, neither quite transparent nor completely opaque, could be located the ribbon straps of her brassiere. "Let me have a few minutes," she coaxed. "I think you might find it a paying proposition."

"Well…" he said. Lust and greed; the double-barreled appeal overcame his caution. When she suggested the privacy of her room at the Freeman he glanced uncertainly into her eyes—and succumbed to that proposal too. Cay began to feel smug. However, Swan remained wary enough to insist that they take a taxi of his own choosing. During the ride she sat close enough to him for his arm to become aware of the softness of her breast. The dying afternoon was hot and the fragrance of sandalwood rose strongly from her in the confinement of the back seat. Swan began to relax perceptibly.

She entered her room first, chatting about nothing. He followed more slowly. With a shamefaced apology, he made certain that they were alone and then bolted both the hall door and the French doors to the balcony. "Cay, I hope you don't mind," he muttered. "I don't mean anything by it."

"Mind that you've locked us up in my bedroom?" She laughed amusedly. "Why, Spencer, who could possibly misinterpret an innocent action like that?" She didn't mind, knowing what she knew: that the screws of the hall-door bolt had been sawed in two so that the bolt would come loose at the slightest pressure; that Rómulo María Felix was stationed in the adjoining room, one of D'Hureau's stethoscopes pressed against the wall, listening.

Swan said solemnly, "I want to believe in you, Cay. But I don't dare trust anything that goes on beyond my senses." He looked at the full bottle of brandy that stood on the chiffonier. "I see. I suppose your next step will be to retire—to slip into something more comfortable, as they say."

"Don't we understand each other, Spencer? I invited you here to discuss business. I don't remember suggesting anything more."

"Don't be angry." He put his hands on her arms. His hands were cold.

"I'm not. However, I must beg to be excused for a moment." She pulled away from him and paused at the bathroom door. "Is it all right? I promise you I won't remove one stitch of clothing while you're my guest."

She closed the door on him, locked it. She had withdrawn for two reasons. First, he was now free to bolster his confidence by going through her belongings, particularly her purse, which she had tossed handily on the farthest bed. Her second reason… From the medicine cabinet she took out a tiny cotton-wrapped hypodermic needle. Gritting her teeth, she averted her eyes and plunged the needle into her upper arm, injecting the small amount of morphine in its glass syringe. The brandy that Swan had eyed so suspiciously was dosed with hyoscine, a drug derived—like scopolamine, the "truth serum"—from atropine. A few drinks would reduce Swan's mental defenses to a babbling fog. D'Hureau had promised her that the prior injection of morphine into her own blood would be sufficient to counteract the excitant quality of the hyoscine. Cay prayed the needle was clean; she had little respect for D'Hureau's habits. Finishing her task with a shudder, she lobbed the hypodermic equipment through the air-shaft transom. Then she flushed the toilet and returned to the bedroom.

From the position of her purse on the bed, she saw that Swan had behaved as she anticipated. He was standing near the glass-paned balcony, his awkward stance limned in the dying sunlight. "You didn't ever expect to see me again," she accused him casually as she switched on a bed lamp.

He immediately and nervously drew the drapes. "I can't make you out, Cay."

"I'm afraid that's not so." She smiled wistfully but didn't approach him. "How dull life would be if we could anticipate it!"

"Is your life ever dull, Cay?"

"Horribly so, sometimes. Even right now, Spencer, with you looking so wound up. You must be an extraordinarily sensitive man."

Swan laughed shortly. "I suppose so. I'm probably off schedule again." He fumbled a small bottle of tablets out of his shirt pocket. "Could I have a glass of water?"

"I'm going to have a brandy."

"Uh, no. Water'll be fine for me. You go ahead if you want to."

"I intend to." She shook her head at him, chuckling. "Are you carrying enough cash to make it worth my while to roll you? Oh, Spencer! What do you think I am, anyway? The bottle isn't even opened yet. See for yourself. I always keep brandy by, glasses too, in case I run into—friends."

"No, I didn't mean you should think—" He wandered closer, guiltily, and looked at the unbroken seal on the bottle; Felix had done a neat job. "I don't know how you always manage to make me feel like a fool, Cay." He opened the bottle and poured two small drinks and they touched glasses. He watched Cay down most of hers before he tried a tentative sip.

"There, the ice is officially broken," she said, and strolled away from him.

He stated slowly, "If it had been left up to me, there wouldn't ever have been any ice. You must believe that I had nothing to do with—the other evening."

She thought: No, don't bother to apologize for your wife's attempted murder. You'll pay for it and so will she. "I believe you, Spencer," she said. "Let's forget it. As one businessman to another, we've both got too much future to worry about."

Without stirring, Swan said, "God, you're beautiful."

She knew that. But Walt Kilmer had paid her that

same compliment in that halcyon afternoon aboard the Rainbow, and swift remorse stung her now. Saturday evening, past six o'clock; Walt would be waiting for her, expecting her footfall on deck any moment. How long would he wait before he gave her up? Oh, wait for me, Walt, please, she implored silently.

Swan sensed something. "You expecting company?" he asked sharply.

"No one. And no one is expecting me, as usual. My time is my own." She artfully wiped her eyes, and he reached for her then. She allowed him to encircle her waist a second before she slipped away. "I don't know about you, but I'm awfully tired of standing." She was telling the truth; the morphine was making her languid. Gracefully, she reclined on the single bed as if it were a chaise longue.

Swan took off his yachting cap with a sudden remembrance of propriety. A sense of urgency throbbed in her but she only stretched luxuriously, heightening her round breasts against the translucent blouse, and let him set the pace. Presently he had to come to her to refill her goblet, and he splashed a greater amount into his own. Then he placed the brandy bottle on the bedstand and sat on the edge of the bed. She had chosen the narrowest bed and their hips touched. His breathing was uneven. He had forgotten about his pills.

"Funny," she said dreamily.

"I don't mean to be, Cay."

"Funny how things work out. No—I take *you* very seriously."

"Do you? You're the first. Or—I guess I'm twisting your meaning."

"Not so much." She sighed as he leaned toward her. She said, "I'm a disciple of direct action, Spencer. What men call forward, in a woman's case. That's why I made certain we'd meet today and talk—like this. Since you admire frankness, I'll go all the way." After a soft pause, "I feel something very deeply. That we need each other."

"I'm no prize," he muttered. "So you must mean the gold."

Cay grimaced. "Your modesty's hard to overcome, isn't it? I can't cope with a man like you—too used to the conceited kind. Sick of them, too. Yes, I'll admit the gold is half of it. I'm human, money's important to me. But, after all, there's happiness too. What kind of life is it when it's dull and empty?" She had worked herself close to genuine tears. "You don't believe me, do you—that I've sometimes had money but nothing to go with it?"

"I can't believe that I—I guess we're all bad off. I—" As he stammered, his arm reached for her and his hand closed fiercely on her shoulder. She flinched but curved her body toward his, closing her eyes. Swan said, "Cay, Cay, tell me what you mean... Don't lie." She lifted her warm mouth and he clumsily found it with his. She drew him tightly against her for a moment, then released him. Shakily Swan stood up. He poured himself another drink and downed it.

She gazed up at him solemnly. "That kiss wasn't a lie, Spencer."

He returned to her embrace, saying hoarsely,

"Concha is nothing to me, not for some time now."

"What does Concha matter? We're the only ones that matter to us. Darling, I need your help so much…"

"What if I were killed?" he asked abruptly. "I might be. I'm the one needing help, Cay—sweetheart. You think my life isn't empty? Oh, if we could only get away, out of this mess. We'd be rich. I could give you things, so many things. I'd give anything to have you love me, real honest-to-God love." It seemed to her almost incredible that she had so easily got Swan to the point of unburdening himself to her. She crooned in his ear, "We'll think of a way out, the two of us, together."

"But the deal has gone pretty far already. Concha wants it that way. What if I were killed? I can't help being afraid of him."

"Who do you mean, darling?"

"Why, the Trader, of—" Swan broke off suddenly and struggled to sit up. "My God, there's somebody coming!"

Cay heard it too, the clatter of the loosened bolt falling on the tiles, her hall door opening. But before she could see past Swan, she heard the intruder's curt voice.

Walt Kilmer was saying, "…couldn't wait all night so I came over to speed you—" He choked off as abruptly as Swan had done, staring dumfounded at the lamplit bed. "What the hell!"

Swan gave a whimper of surprise and scrambled away from her. Cay sat up hastily, her body turning cold. She could see in Walt's shocked eyes the cruel picture of herself, rising in dishevelment from the bed.

"Walt!" she cried miserably. "Why didn't you wait?"

"I sure pulled one, didn't I?" he whispered. His turned-down mouth was pale and sick. "I should've waited my turn like a good customer, instead—"

Cay shrieked, "Walt! No!" but this time it was a warning.

Walt didn't understand and didn't look behind him. His lips were still moving in bitter indictment as Rómulo María Felix stepped through the open hall door, grinning. Felix drove his fist, weighted with rings, into the base of Walt's skull.

Chapter Nineteen

Saturday, December 8, 6:30 P.M.

Felix shut the hall door behind him and stepped across Walt's sprawled body. He held up his ringed fist triumphantly. "I arrive!"

Cay spat. "You couldn't have left things alone. Oh, no!"

Felix' jaw dropped. "You needed a savior. We agreed I should—"

"I didn't need help! I'd have handled it!" Railing at Felix, she realized that she was far from steady. Morphine and hyoscine were using her nerves as their battleground. "Look what you've done to Walt! Look at the mess we're in now!"

Felix looked only at Spencer Swan, who cowered against the chiffonier as if he longed to hide himself in a drawer. The Mexican smoothed his mustache in deprecation. "The situation has complicated," he admitted, "but we still have a firm grasp on our sparrow."

"Oh, be quiet." Cay knelt by Walt and fingered his skull. Nothing was broken. She rose with a fretful sigh and poured a brimming goblet of the brandy. She held it out to Swan, her hand trembling. "I'm sorry, Spencer, but you'll have to drink this."

Swan's cheeks twitched; his eyelids fluttered in horror. "No! You're trying to kill me. How can you, Cay? Lying to me like that, kissing me—"

"Business is business," she interrupted wearily. "Please, I'm not interested in injuring you or your psyche. Simply drink the brandy."

"You're out to kill me," moaned Swan, gray-faced. "You monsters!"

"Be careful about placing ideas in my head," said Felix. He flourished his fist menacingly. "Do as my lady friend advises and drink the brandy!"

Swan grasped the glass in both his hands and, staring at them desperately, drained off the liquor. A trace ran from the corner of his mouth and he fearfully recovered it with his tongue. Cay at once refilled his goblet.

In a low voice, she told Felix, "Now we'll have to go ahead as originally planned. As soon as he's sufficiently under the influence, we'll smuggle him out the back way and over to D'Hureau's. Is the car ready?" And to Swan, she snapped, "Keep at it—drink that one too!"

"I can't," Swan protested weakly, but a snarl from Felix forced the glass to his lips again.

Cay returned bleakly to Walt's unconscious body. Oh, Walt, I shouldn't have involved you with me, she thought. I knew I'd only make you suffer. I've nothing else to give. She prayed for the hyoscine to act quickly on Swan. Walt would come to his senses shortly and Cay didn't intend to let Felix hit him again.

She heard a goblet smash on the floor. She whirled to see Swan, his legs collapsing like soggy cardboard, pitch forward into the astounded arms of Felix. The Mexican dragged him to the bed. "Cay, quickly!" Felix cried. "He looks bad, this one."

"Bad?" she said confusedly. She hurried to Swan, removing his thick spectacles to examine his glassy eyes. The pupils had dilated frighteningly. His pulse rate had mounted so rapidly that Cay couldn't count it. His skin felt hot and dry. She stared across him at Felix' worried face. "D'Hureau didn't tell us to expect this."

"No," whispered the Mexican. "What if he dies? He told us we would kill him, and now here he lies gasping like a fish. I wasn't employed to participate in a murder, *huera*."

"He's not dead yet. Calm down. I can see D'Hureau's mistake. The hyoscine dose—it wouldn't hurt an ordinary man, but it's knocked Swan for a loop. All those pills he takes—he's a sick man, God save us."

"But we can do nothing," Felix said plaintively. "Pardon, I'm leaving you now. I can't bear sickness or death. You summon a doctor, explain this as a heart attack from strenuous love-making. That's best. *Adiós*."

"Stay here," hissed Cay. "We've got to do as I said. Get him down to the car and over to D'Hureau's. If the cops see us, we're finished. D'Hureau claims to be a doctor, and that's what Swan needs." She was already cowling her blue *rebozo* over her head and cramming Swan's yachting cap onto his bushy hair. "Well, *help me!*"

Felix checked the hallway and they supported the limp Swan between them and staggered forth. Walt was stirring as they passed over him but Cay could spare him nothing but a miserable glance. Stumbling often, they doll-walked Swan down the stairs, encountering no one. At the street floor, they turned hastily away from the lobby and its few rocking-chair loungers, and sought the darkness of the rear exit. They groped through a maddening obstacle course of saw horses and cement-mixing troughs and stacks of tile to the rutted alley and the Ford that Felix had rented.

The ride across town, Felix driving, seemed endless. It seemed to Cay that every *mazatleco* was in the streets and each one tried to peer into the Ford's back seat at the man she affectionately clasped in her arms. Swan was still semi-conscious, fast passing into delirium, his feverish lips mumbling pleas for water.

The gloom of the Avenida Rouiles Serdan was leopard-spotted with light from open doorways and grilled windows. Felix parked before the green portal of 477 and they dragged Swan into the unlighted entrance passage. A lamp burning in the living room threw D'Hureau's gross shadow broodingly across the lattice screen.

In his wing chair, he loomed over his small table, and nothing had changed from the day before. His nightly bottle of wine sat half empty on the wood mosaic of the table and beside it lay the cumbersome Lahti automatic. He turned his red-curled head as they hauled Swan into the room but he didn't bother to rise. "Excellent," he intoned. "I had clocked you to arrive at exactly this moment."

"Excellent—rot!" Cay panted. She waved helplessly at Swan's body, prone on the black tiles. "The stuff wasn't supposed to hit him this hard, was it? I think he's dying."

"Nonsense." D'Hureau swallowed the wine in his glass before shoving himself slowly to his feet. "Now let us see." He crouched beside Swan and his silk-gloved hands deftly explored his pulse, his forehead, his eyes. "Very interesting—that your amateurish diagnosis should be right. All the classic symptoms. Rapid pulse, fever, dilation. See, even areas of his skin are turning scarlet. Doubtless, were he fit to question, he could complain of mouth dryness and numb extremities."

"Well, don't just squat there!"

D'Hureau shrugged his freckled shoulders. "Obviously, the stars meant this to happen. Let him die."

Cay didn't argue. One quick step to the table, and then she let D'Hureau stare up into the muzzle of his own gun. "Get to work," she commanded flatly. "Get him well, stars or no stars. Maybe dying men don't affect you, but they do Felix and me."

"We don't mean to offend," wheedled Felix, "but

gold is one thing and murder is far different."

D'Hureau grunted and rose. "Very well. But I shan't forget this atrocity." With Cay and the pistol eying him watchfully, he dragged forth his battered medical kit. The next half hour was tense and ugly, although Cay had to admit that D'Hureau worked with painstaking efficiency. He administered an iodine solution to precipitate the hyoscine in Swan's stomach, followed this with a violent emetic and then hypodermic injections of morphine. When he'd finished, the house reeked, but D'Hureau pronounced the patient out of danger, although he was still in a stupor.

Since nothing more could be gained from Swan, it was decided that Felix would carry the unconscious man back to the Concha, counting on the crew's being absent at the fiesta of the Immaculate Conception.

Felix left. Cay wandered out into the patio and gazed up suspiciously at the stars. Presently D'Hureau joined her, and, with a sigh, she returned his pistol. "Everything's gone wrong," she murmured. "I couldn't help it. Our one small hope is that the Trader may believe we did force Swan to tell us something."

"Forget those ridiculous hopes," growled D'Hureau, thrusting the gun into his pajama waist. "All that's left for us now is force. Tomorrow is Sunday, perhaps our last opportunity, and I shan't let it wither away as tonight has. We must conceive a way to seize the island."

"Without rifles, without transportation? Defeat's making you a little absurd, Doctor. Who'd rent us a boat for a project like that?"

"I'll think of something. By God, I won't be beaten

at this!" He glared up at the night sky and cursed it. "Come see me in the morning, find out if I haven't thought of something! You'll see." He added, sneering, "Provided you and your Mexican don't object to bloodletting."

"A fight's one thing. But to let that man die for no reason—"

"Ha! Integrity should never interfere with income. You and your sudden fine distinctions." He slapped her viciously across the mouth. "Nor can I make distinctions between friend and enemy, when the friend aims a gun at my belly. Never provoke me again."

Cay bent her head wearily and with her handkerchief dabbed at her smeared lipstick. "I've felt all evening I deserved something like that," she said, "though not from you. I'll just take it on account. Have you noticed how far away your stars look tonight?"

Chapter Twenty

Saturday, December 8, 8:00 P.M.

She walked back across town, hunting a vehicle to hire but finding none. To her dope-jangled nerves, the humid night seemed an oppressive burden physically weighting her limbs and she couldn't understand the strange emptiness of the streets at this early hour.

She discovered the reason as she neared the central plaza beneath the rococo spires of the cathedral. What appeared to be the entire population of Mazatlán was pushing its way into the Parque Revolución, blocking the surrounding streets to all but foot traffic. The gay laughing mob, electric with anticipation, thronged everywhere, swarming over the bandstand, surging like a brown tide against the fronts of the post office and the city hall and the church, even perching on the branches of the laurel trees.

Unwillingly, she was caught up into the press of bodies. An infant brother and sister chased each other excitedly around her legs and their black-shawled grandmother apologized and Cay was immediately jostled into the pushcart of a coconut vendor trying to wheel his wares to an unworked lode of customers. Coconuts... Trefethen... She remembered then his telling her not to miss this fiesta. The *mazatlecos* were celebrating the holiday of their patron saint, and Cay found she was joined with them through sheer out-numbering, even infected somewhat by the crowd's animal breath of enthusiasm.

In front of the cathedral had been erected a spindly towering framework as high as a telephone pole, and of garishly decorated birdcage construction. It rose in a series of spheroids to a cluster of four papier-mâché angels who in turn were topped, incongruously, by four bicycle replicas bearing dummy riders. The lofty tower culminated in a star pinwheel. From the level of the angels, four guy wires ran down to stout paper-wrapped posts, some yards away toward each compass point. Each of the posts, twice a man's height, sup-ported a huge crepe-paper ball that gave it the appear-ance of a giant scepter. The people crowded most insistently around the bases of the four scepters.

Grouped within the arched portal of the cathedral, a white-robed boys' choir finished an invocational hymn, while two priests gazed benignly out at the multitude. With the hymn's end came a burst of applause and a shrilly renewed racket of excited children. The general delight was for a self-important man who came marching from the cathedral, holding aloft a smoldering wood brand. The crowd melted away so that he could approach the base of the fiesta tower. He bent down, out of Cay's sight. The mob stilled expectancy.

A hissing sound, a shower of sparks from the lowest spheroid, a loud explosion, and colored fireworks began to whirl and dance within the gaunt framework of the tower. Gaudy flames spun round and round in dazzling patterns. The throng roared approval... and a hand closed cruelly tight about Cay's arm.

"Having more fun?" growled Walt Kilmer angrily.

Her knees weakened. For an instant she was going to let herself press against him, make him embrace her and forgive her. The poignancy of small changes about him struck her now. He had shaved carefully for their broken rendezvous, and he wore a starched white shirt and even a necktie. There had been little time to notice such details during the flurry in her room.

But instead she drew back as far as the pack of people would permit and said dully, "Leave me alone, Walt. Let go of me." Another of the tower's spheroids exploded in fiery display, and then another as the fuse burned upward.

"Maybe you don't want to talk to me, but I want to talk to you." Pyrotechnic colors reflected across his scowling face. "Maybe you've run out of lies—but I don't forget things that easy."

"You shouldn't have come, that's all. I didn't mean for you to be hurt."

"Mighty decent of you. How'd you manage to get a guy behind me, to hit me? What do you do, post a guard before you flop into bed with your friends? Right now I could break your neck."

"*On* the bed, not *in*—" she commenced, then broke off with a whimper. "Oh, what does it matter? I told you from the first to leave me alone. I know, I'm no good, you don't have to tell me." She got her arm free. "Now, go on. I don't want anything to do with you."

His brow furrowed as he stared down at her. "You're still lying," he said, with a bit less antagonism. "The other day you wanted to see me again. Now— What has got you all fouled up, anyway, Cay? I'm mad, sure, but I'll get over that, and you don't even try to talk me out of it."

"Don't come near me again, that's all."

"Are you crazy, Cay? I don't let go like that. If you're in trouble, let me get you out of it."

"You couldn't help me, no one can. Walt, please— good-by."

Whatever he replied was lost in the shouting of spectators. The angels high on the tower had exploded into sparkling brilliance. They began sliding one by one, down the guy wires to the four huge scepters. As the first angel reached his post the crepe paper ball on top unrolled into view a colored lithograph of the Virgin Mary, illuminated by a halo of sparklers. Above the cheering, Walt yelled in her ear, "Damn you, I'm going to help you whether you like it or not!"

Cay gave a dry sob, a last anguished affectionate look into his perplexed eyes, and darted off into the crowd. She heard Walt shouting after her. Her smallness served her well; she was able to wriggle through the massed humanity where he would have difficulty following.

The fourth and final angel passed directly over her head, showering her with harmless silver sparks. The lithographed Virgin made another miraculous appearance. Cay couldn't hear Walt's voice any longer, so she glanced back to be certain she'd lost him. She half stumbled, bumped into a man in her path.

Her apology dried up in her mouth. She was looking into the sleepy slant eyes of Jack Diki. For an instant they stood facing one another in unbreathing surprise. Then Diki's hand stole up to his white silk scarf.

Cay whirled and fled back the way she'd come, this time in panic. She shoved her way blindly through the enraptured onlookers, who paid her no attention. Her first throbbing thought was to put the greatest possible distance between herself and the strangler. But when she looked back, she met his eyes again, his expressionless childish face pursuing her through a multitude of other faces that all grinned upward toward the circle of dummy bicycle riders, now beginning to splutter and blaze and race in a fiery circle.

"Walt," she panted. "Walt, where are you?" She had eluded him too well; perhaps he had given her up as she had insisted. And now that she needed him, her

blurred brain could conceive of no other sanctuary.
"Walt!" The crowd continued shouting at the flaming
bicycle race high overhead. If Diki should catch her
she could be quietly garroted in the midst of thou-
sands of people and no one would notice until his soft
hands let her fall to the ground.

Suddenly she had burst through to the fringes of
the throng and, at a run, struck off along a dark street
toward the taxi stand a block away.

She reached the row of battered cabs and sobbed in
disappointment. Not a driver, not an ignition key
among them. All were somewhere in the crowd she
had run away from. She gasped at the sound of soft
quick footsteps. Behind her, along the high shadowy
sidewalk, Diki advanced inexorably.

Cay stared around desperately. Across the intersection, the colossal iron-roofed bulk of the public market
seemed to beckon to her. The huge building filled an
entire city block, its encircling arcade bounding a
jungle of shops and stalls, all deserted for the night.
Surely in that labyrinth she could find a hiding place.
She sprinted across the intersection, making as little
noise as possible in her high heels. She cursed her
shoes. She cursed D'Hureau and the drugs that were
slowing her mind and body.

Her luck turned worse. As she reached the steps in
the opposite curb, the whole sky abruptly blazed red.
The fuse had finally burned to the pinnacle of the fireworks tower, and the pinwheel star, shooting high
above the spires of the cathedral, spun radiantly overhead, banishing all friendly shadows.

The ramshackle arcades offered a tunnel of darkness but no practical concealment now that Diki had sighted her again. She sped along the gloomy corridor anyway, expecting any moment to see his willowy silhouette appear in the arcade entrance. When it seemed to her that he was long overdue, she shrank aside between two sugary bake-stall counters. She was just in time; the next moment she heard his gentle step in the arcade.

The walls of the market proper consisted of brick pillars alternating with stretches of iron grating. Making herself tiny against the chilly bars, she discovered that two of them were bent slightly apart. Another whisper of Diki's prowling footsteps, and Cay slipped inside the market.

She was among straw hats of all shapes and sizes, piled on benches, racked on shelves. Cay crept around a table and out of the hat shop and into a girder-ceilinged vault of a thousand odors: fresh leather and rancid meat and sweat and stale cooking. On every side stood goblin shapes, worktables with mysterious objects covered for the night, counters and stands piled with familiar objects weird in their absolute desertion. From seeing the market in daylight, she knew of its several entrances. All she had to do was reach the opposite side and let herself out before Diki could follow.

She glided past mounds of unwashed vegetables and pillars of nested baskets; she ducked under heavy fringes of suspended pottery and weaved through a series of mess tables that served as a restaurant. She peered about uncertainly; this night-shrouded place was far larger than the market she had seen by day.

A rocket from the plaza cast its radiance through the lofty skylights, brightening her surroundings with the quick brilliance of a lightning bolt. She choked back a scream. The sudden flash had brought her face to face with a white skull, gazing at her like the accusing ghost of Eduardo Valdes. Then she recognized it as a toyshop's painted mask, left over from last month's Day of the Dead. A far worse fright was the clattering sound behind her as someone's groping hand brushed an object to the floor.

But the rocket showed her briefly the nearest gate. With quaking hands she felt her way over to its iron bars, sought for the latch—and her nervous fingers met a large padlock. She couldn't see well enough to experiment with it, and there was the possibility of noise. She remained calm enough to relinquish a lost cause quickly. She moved quickly along the aisle through the stench of butcher's blocks. She ducked as another rocket lit up the interior of the building; her steadying hand came down upon a cold slab of raw meat and her stomach turned over.

A third rocket exploded over the market's iron roof. This time she saw Diki, advancing across the cluttered floor, eyes roving back and forth in search of her. His scarf dangled from his hands.

Bending low, Cay crept to the second gate. Her prayers went unanswered; it was padlocked as firmly as the first. The terrible truth caught up with her: The only exit was the accidental way she had entered, and only God knew where that was now, and Diki was unknowingly barring her path. In a sudden burst of panic, she rattled the iron bars of the gate. It refused to yield. The market was no sanctuary; instead, it had become a huge cage.

Another rocket burst, and she had no place to hide. She froze before the gate, hoping the afterglow would fade before Diki discovered her. He stood a scant twenty yards away, his seeking face slowly turning toward her. The rocket snuffed out and she breathed again.

And at that instant, a bus chugged down the street, playing its headlights full upon her, outlining her clearly against the bars. In that momentary nightmare of light, she saw the gleam of Diki's lidded eyes, saw him moving forward. Then returning darkness left her with only a memory of a sheen of white silk. Held throat high, it was floating down the aisle toward her.

She felt very tired, not like fighting at all, although of course she had to fight because she had always fought. It seemed a little stupid that all she had made of herself should end this way, a dreadful waste of talent.

Diki was coming through the dark. Already she had detached her blackjack from her purse. Her left hand, intuitively exploring, discovered on a glass showcase a cardboard rack of tiny cheap penknives. She thumbed one of the feeble blades open and, with a weapon in each hand, waited with her back against the locked gate. Make it a good fight, anyway, she told herself at the same time she was wondering what had happened to her usually invulnerable hope.

She crouched slightly, braced against the strangler's final rush. Where was he? Then she sensed that Diki was no longer moving toward her. "Well, come on," she dared him between her teeth.

Behind her, from outside the gate, Walt said, "Cay, is that you? You all right?"

She sagged against the iron bars, felt his strong hands reach through and catch at her shoulders. "Walt, Walt," she whispered, and he was actually touching her, his breath on the back of her head.

Another rocket spread its bright plumes through the sky. A dim quick glow—but Diki had vanished. Cay said, "I think I'll be all right now," and turned around to face Walt, to smile weakly at him through the bars. But for his grip on her, she would have fallen to the ground.

Chapter Twenty-One

Saturday, December 8, 9:00 P.M.

"Hold on, honey. Get you out in a second." Walt hooked his thumbs in the padlock hasp. She heard his breath suck in, saw the tendons stand out on the backs of his hands. Then the padlock snapped open, and the iron gate swung outward and she slid into his arms. He stroked her hair, holding her tightly, and murmured reassurances against her cheek. Now that her extreme fright had passed, her strength dissolved.

"I thought I was done for sure," she said, "when that bus turned its lights on me. And those skyrockets kept—"

"You don't know how lucky that bus was for you. I thought I'd seen you heading in this direction but I didn't suspect you were inside the market. I was giving up looking for you, when those bus lights…" His voice changed; he spoke softly but no longer tenderly. "Seems I got a little unfinished business with that guy who was after you. He's still inside there."

"No," she begged him. "No, he'll be gone by now. Walt, don't leave me alone again." He grunted and agreed reluctantly. They walked slowly back toward the plaza, through the dissipating crowd of pedestrians and vehicles.

But when she grabbed his elbow suddenly he swung around quickly with a tense "What's wrong?" and she murmured, "Nothing—nothing. I'm jumping at shadows." It had been more than a shadow, the taxi cruising by them, the handsome savage face of Concha Swan gazing at her from the dark interior, a sudden glimpse as startling as the skull mask in the market. Cay wasn't certain that the encounter was accidental. She didn't want to think about it. For the moment, she didn't have the strength to fight any more.

They found an *araña* for hire. Cay supposed they would go to the Rainbow, but, after Walt's muttered instructions to the driver, the *araña* turned away from the harbor. "Where are you taking me, Walt?"

"A place," he said briefly. "You'll see."

She leaned against him in the bumping gig and didn't worry about more questions. They rolled through the town and wound their way up the dirt streets of the Cerro de la Nevería; this Hill of the Ice House marked the mainland end of Mazatlán's peninsula as the Cerro del Vigía did the seaward end. Below them winked the lights of the city and the only sound was the measured thump of the horse's hoofs. Cay closed her eyes.

Through her peaceful half sleep, Walt said, "Here it is, darling." The *araña* had stopped. Cay raised her head from his shoulder. On the crest of the hill, they had halted before a tiny frame cottage, its unpainted sides and shed roof acrawl with lush green vines. It resembled a nursery-tale bush with doors and windows, and it stood quite alone among a grove of star-leaved mango trees.

Walt paid off the driver and helped her alight. As the *araña* trundled off down the hill, he kept his hands at her waist. She lifted her questioning face and he said, "I rented it two days ago."

He led her along the path to the vine-burdened porch and found a key in his pocket and unlocked the door. She waited in the doorway while he lit two kerosene lanterns. They cast a dim yellow glow about the single room, befriending the primitive furnishings: a monolithic iron range with rickety flue, a handmade varnished wooden table with two chairs, a chipped white iron-frame bed that was neatly made up with blankets Cay thought she recognized from the Rainbow. She walked over and fingered the bouquet of yellow hibiscus in a vase on the table. She felt she had to say something, he was expecting it. She murmured, "Funny little house. No, I don't mean that—I mean it's so *clean.*"

He was nervous. He spoke too harshly. "Hell, yes, it ought to be. I been scrubbing on my hands and knees for the last two days. To make it fit for—" He stopped.

She turned to gaze softly at his stiff face. "Why, Walt?"

"Well, I thought the Rainbow was kind of small and ugly for what I had in mind. I got a sense of proportion." He shrugged. "Might as well tell you, you can guess anyway. The boat just didn't seem right for it."

Cay gaped. Then she thought of scoffing at him and his phony-ingenuous line. But she dropped her eyes quickly. She was realizing that the rarefied subtleties of her own career had all but spoiled her for anything but subtlety. Walt wasn't stringing her at all; in his direct and brutal fashion he was simply not concealing anything from her.

He said, "What are you thinking?"

"Nothing. I was just looking at the outhouse there in the back yard. It's all covered with bougainvillea, all royal purple." She giggled foolishly. "Have you ever seen a prettier one in all your life?"

"You weren't thinking about that."

She spun around and went to him swiftly. "If anything, I'm a little surprised you thought I needed a setting." Happily she responded to his arms convulsively clamped around her. "Nearer," she said. "Don't let me breathe." She stroked his intent face until it smiled a little.

"I don't want to hurt you, Cay."

"I don't want to hurt you, Walt. That's why you've got to understand about what happened tonight."

"Shut up," he commanded brusquely. "For a minute now I've got you. I don't want to louse it up with talk, that long speech about how no good you are." He kissed her. She raised herself on her toes, pushing herself upwards against his hard body until her lips touched his.

"I feel wonderfully good now," she said softly. She wanted him, she couldn't remember ever wanting a man so much. But what about later when her flesh and her fear and her loneliness were assuaged? Could she remain in contentment then—or would her mind go on with its sly addition and subtraction, making certain that the ledger sheet always showed a favorable balance for Cay Morgan?

Walt said, "All you need is a little taking care of. I'm going to take care of you. You're my woman, you were cut out to be. I've never run across anything like you before. I knew the second I saw you. I'm no kid, Cay, but you scared me at first, meaning so much so quick. Why are you crying? It's nothing to cry about."

"Walt, kiss me. I love you."

"And I love you, Cay. I've never been like this before. Never so damn happy. Why can't you be?"

"I can. I am." She rubbed her face against his shirt, drying her eyes. "It's just that I don't want to think any more." Their mouths locked again. Against his lips she murmured, "Put out the lamps, Walt."

"Why? I want to look at you."

"Please, darling. For my sake."

His hand came slowly to her face. Deliberately, he pushed aside the screen of hair that hid the ugly T scar. "Because of this?" he asked quietly.

She went rigid in his arms, searching his eyes. "You shouldn't have done that, Walt. I was trying to forget, but now I can't. I didn't want you to see me like that, not tonight. I was pretending I was no different than any other woman."

"You are different. You're more beautiful."

"Don't lie to me, please. I know how I look, how revolting it is. Like seeing a crippled man; it does something to you. Men are bound up in their strength, women in their beauty. That's the way of nature."

"We did enough pretending on the boat." He bent and gently kissed her forehead over and over. "It's a very little scar," he whispered. "It's inside you've let it get so deep. I love a lot more about you than what I can see or touch, don't you understand that?"

"Walt," she said, "my whole life is pretending."

"You said you loved me."

"That was genuine. The only genuine things about me: my love—and my hate." She sighed. "Darling, there's no choice now, either mine or yours. You've got to know about my past."

"What's a past? I've got one of sorts."

"Not like mine. I lied to you on the boat, Walt. My parents weren't wealthy. They didn't leave me even a memory. And I'm in Mazatlán for a reason, just as I've been everywhere in the last five years for a reason. I came here to find a man, someone I've been hunting to the ends of the earth. Five years ago I was in Morocco..." and she told him the story. About smuggling antique jewelry, about Eduardo Valdes and her defiance of the Trader, and how she had been punished for that defiance. "He drugged me and kidnaped me and taught me the lesson I'd been promised. Something worse than death."

His eyes narrowed. "The scar—"

"Not a scar. A brand. Not beaten or tortured—but branded! What worse could happen to a woman? To be disfigured, branded like cattle, to wear *his* mark for the rest of my life!" Her voice was rising shakily and years of hate twisted her lips. "The Trader marked me for all time. That's why I can never forget! I'm branded as something of his—and I'll never be free until I kill him!"

He pulled her face against his chest to muffle her words and he held her trembling figure with fingers that bruised cruelly. Above her head his voice grated, "Get this straight: You're not killing anybody."

She tried to shake loose but he held her. "I am! It's all that's kept me going! It's all I have!"

"Look at me," he commanded. She looked at him, and his face was a frightening sinewy mask. "You've got something else now. Me. I'm yours and you're mine. I've taken you over and I've taken over your debts. I'm not asking you to give up anything. But from now on, I pay the bills for both of us."

"No, Walt! Afterward, I can come to you, belong to you truly—"

His hand went out to the table, picked up his long-barreled revolver that lay there. "This belongs to me. So do you. I'll handle you both." He put the gun back and pulled her slowly to his chest, showing her his brutal strength. "Do you believe me?"

She felt his mouth master her, felt her resolve melting into his reservoir of male power. She cried desperately, "I want to believe you! Oh, how much I want to believe you!"

"I'll show you." He released her and went to the lanterns on the wall. His eyes locked with hers, he said, "Now we can put out the lights, like normal people, for the normal reasons." She held out her arms to the darkness, and he found her.

"Beautiful," he said. "Any time—in the light or in the dark—you're the most beautiful woman in the world. And you're mine."

"Yes," she said. "Yes, my darling,"

I've needed you always, her trembling form implored him, and even as she clasped him to her she thought joyously, I belong to somebody, at last I belong to somebody!

Chapter Twenty-Two

Sunday, December 9, 8:00 A.M.

The idea possessed her the instant she awoke. She couldn't be sure that she hadn't dreamed it.

Over the side of the bed Cay could see the sunlight and vine shadows on the floor; beyond that, the long shape of Walt's revolver on the rough table. She lay gazing steadily at the revolver. "It's Sunday," she murmured aloud. Sunday, the ninth of December, the Trader's last day for something—perhaps her final chance, too.

She rolled over swiftly, whispering, "Walt," to awaken him. He only blinked drowsily and she flung herself upon him, kissing the mouth she had once thought cynical. "Walt, wake up. I want to tell you something."

He chuckled, folding himself about her. "I love you. Afraid I'd forgotten?" His hand stroked her back.

"Oh, and I love you so much!" she said vehemently. "But let me alone for a minute, darling. I have something to tell you." She captured his wandering hand and kissed it thoroughly, even to the cameo ring on its little finger.

Walt had stopped smiling at her. He said, "If it's about that—" he glanced at her bangs—"don't forget I said I pay the bills."

"I'm not doubting your ability," Cay said. "And, darling, you'll never know how deeply I've changed, loving you as much as I do. But please don't treat me as a nice soft stay-at-home toy. I'm a grown woman, I'm a thinking person, never forget. For example, how do you propose to—pay this bill?"

Into his gray eyes came a sullen uncertainty. She nudged comfortably closer to him and said, "Then suppose I tell you all the rest of it, darling. Then we can work it out together." She related the details. He was not impervious to the imminence of the fortune in Spanish ingots, although she became more excited telling about it than he did, hearing of it for the first time. Money always aroused her. "D'Hureau mentioned an idea yesterday that might be brazen enough to succeed. He wants to sail over and seize the island." She paused. "But D'Hureau doesn't have a boat. That's what I was thinking about, darling."

"Yeah," said Walt slowly. "I see. I've been fishing those waters. The Rainbow could make an approach without raising suspicion. Maybe they wouldn't expect an open attack, not from a low-class bucket like the Rainbow."

"We must consider the high odds, of course, Walt. The Swans aren't much, but there's the Trader and Diki and whoever else he might have—and the plantation workers have rifles now, I'm certain."

He lay silent for a while, staring up at the ceiling. "Do you realize, Cay, if that gold is really there and we can locate it—well, think what that'd mean to you and me. We could really settle down, really live a normal life, just love and be rich."

"That's what I want," she whispered passionately. "An end to wandering. Not that it would be wandering if it was with you. Home is where the husband is." She nuzzled her face into the hollow of his shoulder. "Oh, to be able to do this always."

His arms tightened. His voice said huskily against her hair, "You started this."

"Walt, we don't have time." But she felt her blood rekindled and she surrendered convulsively.

Later, as her heartbeats slowed in languid rest, she became conscious of time ticking away inexorably. So, despite his protests, Cay dressed quickly and taxied into the city alone. The cathedral chimes were heralding the ten-o'clock mass as she arrived at Avenida Rouiles Serdan 477.

She didn't see Felix, but D'Hureau was his customary heavy-headed silhouette against the lattice screen. He stared at her with morose animosity as she strode into the living room. "I've thought of nothing," he admitted distastefully. "Even thinking all night, I've found no way for us to reach the island."

Cay said, "Brace yourself. I've got a safe boat to use." She told him a little about the Rainbow.

Exhilaration reddened his freckles. But he said suspiciously, "This Kilmer—what does he expect out of it?"

She told him and the argument began. The cords stood out on D'Hureau's throat as he raved at her in French. She laughed silkily. He brandished his pistol and she coolly lit a cigarette. She imagined how Walt would laugh if he could hear her demands; they were all her own idea, because she couldn't resist a bargain. "Better rest your blood pressure, D'Hureau," she announced flatly, "because that's how the spoils will be divided. My original terms—half to you, half to Walt and me. You pay Felix from your share. You see, you're merely an extra convenience to me now. Times have changed. Now I have the brains *and* the muscle *and* the boat."

He stood up, gloved fists clenched. "You thief of a devil! Why did I ever set eyes on your leprous white face, that hair like pond scum—"

"Quit crying. If your story is true, half the gold will be more than you'll ever live to spend." She added cheerfully, "Besides, the Trader might kill you and solve all your problems."

"Or he might kill you and your man," D'Hureau snarled. He sank to his chair in sour silence. Cay waited him out patiently. Finally he grumbled, "Very well, I am cornered by your sudden possession of a safe boat. But I agree only if we can make the attack tonight."

"I'm aware of the date as well as you. But we need guns." She kept as her secret the existence of Walt's .45 revolver. "That Lahti of yours isn't enough."

"I have a source for rifles," said D'Hureau. "Kindly

observe I do have my values." Cay pulled over the ottoman and they sat making plans for a while. Felix would be notified, and the three of them would rendezvous at D'Hureau's house at sundown, preparatory to proceeding with the rifles to the Rainbow, where Walt would be waiting for them. They decided the attack should be frontal, the Rainbow mooring at the pier on Swan's very doorstep.

Cay hastened back to the cottage. Walt blinked when he heard about it. "I thought these things took days! You sure your buddy can produce the rifles by six o'clock? Look—I got to get a full load of gas aboard our bucket, and we want those engines tuned to a fare-thee-well for a job like this."

"It's got to be tonight. That letter I found on Valdes' body spoke of the ninth of December as some sort of deadline. Well, today is the ninth. Tomorrow the Trader might be miles away. I might never be this close to him again."

He grinned and kissed her roughly. "Then tonight we go. Don't worry, honey, you'll have your Trader's head on a platter, and a million bucks besides."

"Much more than a million, darling." Proudly she explained the new concessions she had forced from D'Hureau. "But he's got to be watched closely, especially after we locate the gold pit. He made a great deal of noise but he let go a bit too easily. I'm certain he's got other plans."

"He's not the only one," Walt said, and kissed her again.

After he'd gone, Cay puttered around the cottage, reluctant to leave it when she knew they would probably never return here again. Yet with Walt gone, the magic was gone also, and shortly after noon she closed the door behind her.

No messages awaited her at the Hotel Freeman. She wondered briefly about Leonard Trefethen, so persistently attentive at first but now entirely vanished from her orbit.

She lay down in her room, but found it impossible to nap. The afternoon gradually dragged by, like a slow-burning fuse that led to the powder keg of night. *Tonight*... Her heart pounded a little. *After five years... tonight!*

The sun dipped nearer the brassy ocean. She arose and dressed herself in dark blue slacks, a matching pullover sweater and jacket. The outfit's warmth was uncomfortable now but that would prove a virtue on the sea at night. Over her shining hair she tied a black silk bandanna; she slipped her feet into low boots of soft leather. She chose, for its capacity, the inexpensive straw purse that Walt had bought her. She put in it her blackjack and a dark pair of wide-cuffed doeskin gloves.

With a last tense smile a her piratical image in the mirror, she opened the door to leave.

Concha Swan, in black, stood only a yard away in the hall. In the dimness, Cay's brain registered two gleaming points—in Concha's shadowed countenance the bestial baring of her teeth, and in her hand a stubby wide-mouthed bottle. The hand jerked up, the bottle pointed, and its dose of watery liquid streamed through the air toward Cay's astounded face.

She thrust up her purse to shield herself and felt the acid sear into her flesh.

Chapter Twenty-Three

Sunday, December 9, 6:00 P.M.

The straw purse fell to the tiles. For an instant, Cay reeled dizzily at the horror of what had happened to her—no, *nearly* happened, for the agony localized itself to burning streaks across two fingers of her still outthrust hand. Her face was unharmed, only two fingers splashed. At her feet the oil of vitriol fumed hungrily over the straw fibers of the big purse that had saved her.

Concha Swan didn't move. She seemed as shocked as Cay. The empty bottle dropped from her limp hand and broke on the floor. She shuddered convulsively at the sound, whispering in Spanish, "I waited, I waited so long for you, you bleach-haired she-goat. I want to hear you scream, but you stand there unhurt." She shook her head, a frown of utter incredibility contorting her strong features.

"I don't scream," Cay said, "but we'll see about you." She sprang across the pool of acid and clawed one hand into Concha's black braided hair, the other at her proud bosom. She flung Swan's wife against the wall.

Even as she sprang at her again, Cay felt a new sense of surprise about Spencer Swan. She had never imagined that Concha would care what he did, including his miserable adventure in Cay's room, but Concha did care. Some unknown quantity about Swan made Concha care deeply enough to attack any rivals.

The Mexican woman was the larger, but she had less experience in gutter fighting. She tried to scratch like a cat. Cay knocked up her arms, stepped in with a heeled hand to her chin and a viciously low blow to her body. "She-goat," gasped Concha, bending with pain.

Cay smiled hideously and dragged her erect by her hair. She drove her free set of knuckles into Concha's right eye. Then she lifted her knee and threw all her weight into the woman's body again. Concha's red mouth opened wide in a soundless spasm. "Twice you've tried for me," panted Cay. "How do you like it?" Sidestepping the raking nails again, she hammered short stabbing blows into the firm-mounded targets of Concha's breasts. Concha tried to spit on her and Cay felt the saliva on her fist as she hit her in the mouth. Then she grabbed hold of the black dress and lingerie beneath and deliberately ripped everything down to the waist. The sight of that tawny skin enraged Cay further; her own fair flesh had been intended to be a scab-encrusted seared monstrosity. She reached out sharp hands for Concha's handsome face.

Then she stepped back quickly as the elevator doors rattled. Out sauntered a middle-aged American couple; one of the hotel boys carried their luggage. As they passed, Cay and Concha were merely two women who had paused in conversation. Two women breathing heavily, an ember-dyed blonde and a tousled brunette who leaned against the wall, hands clasped tightly at the top of her dress.

The elevator boy used his key on the door opposite and let the Americans enter.

"In a moment," said Cay softly. "In another moment."

They glared at each other. Concha straightened, gathering her strength. The Mexican boy came out of the room, gave them a glance, and returned to his elevator. He paused and faced them politely. "Will either of you ladies be wishing to descend?"

"*No, gracias,*" said Cay at the same time that Concha said, "*Sí, por favor.*" The boy waited while the two women exchanged final low-voiced amenities. "The next time," promised Concha between lips that were beginning to swell, "I'll dispose of you so that no man will ever want to look at you again."

"You're looking ill," Cay chided grimly. "Perhaps you *had* better run away now. Perhaps if you got some fresh air, my dear—down on the streets you know so well…" She sent a mocking laugh after Concha, who was already stalking toward the elevator, still holding her dress together in front.

Cay plucked up her straw purse by one corner and hurried into her room and sat down shakily on the bed. She turned slow questioning eyes toward the mirror. Her face was paler than normal, but untouched. For a few minutes, remembering what might have been, she thought she might be sick. She poured herself a brandy instead.

Finally she realized that time was passing. She went into the bathroom and poured milk of magnesia over her burned fingers. The injured areas were small, not enough to incapacitate her. Her doeskin gloves had escaped unscathed. She drew them on. Her plaited blackjack and other items were salvageable, so she transferred them to the smaller tan suede purse and tossed the straw ruin into the air shaft.

This time she opened the hall door warily. No one waited to ambush her there or downstairs. She popped into the nearest taxi and gave the address on the Avenida Rouiles Serdan.

The avenue was dark with the dying twilight. But once through the unlocked green door and into the entrance hall, Cay saw the lamps burning in the living room. D'Hureau's gross shadow showed against the screen at the end of the passage. His bottle sat on the shadow table before him but there was no sign of Felix. "It's Cay," she called out, rounding the screen. "Sorry I'm late, but—" She grasped the screen for support. Both D'Hureau and Felix were there waiting for her—in a grisly fashion. Neither of them moved or would ever move again, she knew that instantly. D'Hureau still sat upright in his wing chair, his red head lolled forward. Cay could see the cold perspiration still dotting his freckled cheeks. Clenched in his lap, he held his wineglass yet, but the wine had spilled and soaked into his white duck trousers. Felix' glass lay where it had rolled under the table. He sprawled face down on the floor, one arm extended rigidly as if pointing accusingly at her.

Cay put her hand over her eyes and took several deep breaths. She opened her eyes again, knowing that death's charade would still be before them. Without hope she walked unsteadily to the table and raised D'Hureau's head. His eyes stared glassily at her

and there was froth on his lips. She caught the bitter
odor of cyanide. She pulled off a glove and touched his
wrist. His flesh still remained warm. It was a warm
evening. She shivered.

She didn't put herself through the ordeal of examining Felix too; there was no need. Looking at
D'Hureau's nightly bottle of wine on the table in front
of him, Cay say the picture clearly. The bottle was only
about a third empty; say, one glass for each of them.
Somehow, the Trader had finally located the traitorous
D'Hureau. Possibly Spencer Swan had remembered
more from his hyoscine nightmare than they had
believed possible. The Trader would have known all
his ex-employee's habits, including the sundown ritual
of the wine. So it was, Cay concluded bitterly, simply a
grim duplication of their own treatment of Swan. The
Trader had seen to it that D'Hureau's entire stock of
wine was poisoned and resealed. When?

Stacked against the patio wall were four rifles, old-
fashioned British Enfields. D'Hureau must have left
his refuge to acquire them. Then it had been during
his absence that the poisoner had paid his visit.
Glancing upward through the open patio, she envi-
sioned Diki creeping insect-like across the flat
rooftops to accomplish his grim errand.

Cay shivered again. What if she had *not* been late
for the rendezvous? What if Concha Swan had *not*
interfered? Then she would have joined her two
companions in wine—and in death. She clapped her
hand to her mouth, stifling a hysterical laugh.
Concha's luck had been doubly bad; not only had she
failed with the acid, but she had also prevented Cay

from keeping an appointment with the Trader's cyanide.

Cay listened then to the stillness of the house. Of course, she was alone. The Trader had been sure that poison would claim her as well as the two men. With a steady hand she reached down for the Lahti automatic in D'Hureau's belt and drew it free. His body shifted slightly but didn't topple. She was able to wedge the pistol into her suede purse. Here, at least, she had made a gain. For the first time in five days she possessed a gun.

She tiptoed into the patio. The platano tree looked much like the banana tree beside it, but she found the hole bored in it. She felt in the cavity and a second later, smiling crookedly, she held the blackened lump of gold in her hand. The poisoner hadn't dared take time to search it out.

Cay glanced fearfully into the lighted living room at her two dead associates. Walt was impatiently awaiting them aboard the Rainbow, ready for the foray against the island. Could the remaining two of them attempt it now? Cay eyed the four Enfields longingly but hopelessly. Her purse was already a burden with pistol and gold. She couldn't carry even one rifle without attracting attention.

A sudden sound from the living room stabbed terror through her. She fumbled at her purse, trying to free the pistol, before she recognized the musical chime of D'Hureau's wrist watch striking the hour of seven.

She waited until the chime had stopped striking. Then she left the patio, walked swiftly through the living room and out the passageway to the front door.

She badly needed the strength of Walt's arms about her; together they would think up the next right move.

Cay closed the street door behind her. She looked about; no one was near on the dark avenue. Keeping to building shadows, she headed for the corner and the taxi parked there. "I want to go to the harbor front, El Muelle. Quickly, please!"

From in back of her, a hand descended upon her arm. Leonard Trefethen's clipped voice advised, "That's not the proper move at all, my girl."

Chapter Twenty-Four

Sunday, December 9, 7:00 P.M.

She turned slowly. He let go of her arm, smiling diffidently. His shirt collar lay open with just the right air of carelessness, and he wore well-tailored white coat and trousers, which made him ghostly against the backdrop of shadows. There was no time for her to unleash her newly stolen pistol, but the purse's heavy load made it a sort of weapon, if necessary.

"Did I frighten you?" drawled Trefethen. "I didn't mean to."

"You meant to, but you didn't. Am I to consider this interference?"

"My dear Cay, you're nippy this evening!" He looked genuinely contrite. "I was calling on you at the Freeman just as you scampered out. I considered my call important enough to tag along."

"I don't need any soap, thank you, and I'm in a hurry, if you'll excuse me."

"Perhaps you shouldn't be." He paused for effect, then winked affectionately. "Say, I find that trousers outfit you're wearing absolutely charming. I'd've followed such a backside around the world—whether I had important business with you or not."

Cay said tautly, "I am in a hurry, Leonard. If you have business, out with it."

"Nerves, nerves," he warned her gently. "To set you at rest, I'll have this taxi follow close behind us as we meander. Have no fears for your safety."

"Much to your surprise, I'm not the least frightened."

"Oh, I didn't mean you should have fears of *me*." Trefethen leaned into the taxi, instructed the driver. The cab, headlights dimmed, rolled slowly behind them as they strolled the gloomy sidewalk, Cay fretting with restless urgency. Trefethen cozily linked their arms.

He chuckled. "You didn't fall for the soap story, did you? I give you credit for having more sense than to believe my interest in Swan was caused by his coco oil."

"I believe in nothing."

"Nor do I. See how much alike we are, Cay? We both live by stratagem and by other people's foolish confidence. I knew we were a pair when I caught you in my room, eavesdropping on the Swans. I did worry about you that tragic evening, but I didn't dare tip my own hand, did I? First rule of the game."

"I think I understand you," Cay said softly. "Confidence?"

"My talents are as varied as yours, my dear. Needless to say, we've both come to Mazatlán after the same golden lure. Don't look so surprised at my admitting it. The story of the gold is a poorly kept secret, very. By this time, rumors of it have spread all over the Americas—at least, in our set."

"Don't be fool enough to warn me off, then."

"Oh, dear Cay!" He stopped walking and faced her quizzically. "Quite the contrary. I've had a potent interest in you ever since we met under such delicious circumstances. Remember the towel?" Tenderly he stroked her jacketed arm. "Much of me is terribly genuine, my dear. We seek the same reward, so why not form a partnership?"

"In other words, you need help."

"I could use a partner. To be as frank as the little animals"—he toyed with the collar of her sweater, his fingers touching her throat lightly—"I think we could have loads of fun together, in every way."

Cay gravely removed his hand. "Sorry, Leonard. I appreciate the offer and knowing where we stand. But I'm all tied up—permanently."

"Permanently? Ah." He pursed his lips and his mustache bristled in wry amusement. He shoved his hands languidly into his pockets. "Then let me ask you a question or two. Have you ever inspected the engines aboard Mr. Kilmer's shabby little fishing boat?"

She gasped. "Walt? How do you know…? No."

"They're amazingly powerful. Have you ever examined his radio apparatus? Did you discover the rifle compartment beneath the port bunk below decks?"

She whispered, "My God, *what are you saying?*"

Trefethen frowned faintly. "My turn to be sorry for you, then. You see, I've known Kilmer from before, in the States. Hence my friendly warning. I'm quite afraid he may also know me. There was some nasty trouble. Cay, dear, Kilmer was and undoubtedly still is an agent of the United States government, Treasury Department."

"I don't believe you! I can't—"

"It's my guess that Federal Agent Kilmer is working co-operatively with the Mexican government to track down Swan's treasure. The good old U.S.A. probably fears—no doubt with good reason—that the Trader will dispose of the gold to Peking or some other unfriendly power. That's merely a guess…"

His casual voice ran on dimly through the roaring in Cay's head. The sidewalk seemed to tilt and she squeezed shut her eyes. One phrase throbbed in her ears: federal agent. She tried to speak the appalling fact aloud: "My lover is a *cop!*" but she had no voice. Cay Morgan, who broke every law but her own, had given herself, heart and body, to a policeman. How could she believe it? Yet how not, when it all fitted together in cruel perfection? Walt's boat sailing so fortuitously near Swan's island the night he rescued her. Trefethen avoiding her after seeing her with Walt. Walt's persistence in courting her, his alacrity in joining her—and D'Hureau and Felix—in their quest for the gold, his readiness to learn their plans…

Cay moaned. Surely the gold had not been all. What of herself and Walt? Their passion, their dreams of the future—had *everything* of theirs all been tricks of his, the lies of a cop probing her secrets?

"It can't be true. It can't," she mumbled dully.

Trefethen misunderstood. "I'm certain I'm not mistaken. It was less than three years ago I ran afoul of this chap who now calls himself Kilmer—in San Francisco, a matter of postal notes. Cay, where are you going?"

She was already running back toward the taxi. The driver held open the door and she tumbled inside, saying to herself, I've got to ask him. I've got to hear him say it. When the driver inquired something about the water front, she nodded vacantly and sank back as the taxi jerked into gear. She caught a last blurred glimpse of Trefethen, hands still pocketed, standing in slouched dismay on the sidewalk.

Cay sat up stiffly as the taxi rolled onto the concrete wharving, its puzzle of masts and rigging swaying mysteriously against the night sky. Lighted portholes of some of the boats glowed at her like cats' eyes. She had the driver cruise the length of the water front twice before she got out and dismissed him. The Rainbow was not there!

She made the same journey on foot, peering at the unwieldy silhouettes of fishing smacks and barges, questioning every person she met. At last she encountered a sailor who remembered. He had noticed a dark blue boat with a white stripe put out through the harbor channel at sundown.

She returned dazedly through the dark to the empty few yards of water where the Rainbow had been docked. Nearby lay a fresh-smelling stack of lumber, roped for loading. Cay wearily seated herself on the planks and stared at the vacant berth, listened to the sibilant laughter of tiny waves. The truth slowly twisted itself into a knot in her brain.

Walt—the federal agent, the *cop*—had never intended to help her and D'Hureau carry out the invasion plans. That was clear. No wonder he had been surprised at the speed of the plan; that speed had forced his hand. Walt had been trapped into ending his game of watching, waiting, spying. Cay whimpered as she thought of what she had driven him to do. Alone, he had sailed to the island in his own bold last-ditch attempt to locate the gold before one side or the other could remove it.

He must have loved me, he must have, Cay told herself frantically. He couldn't have been lying about everything, not about us. Oh, Walt darling, why didn't you tell me? Please come back and tell me.

The night crawled sluggishly by as she sat there in the shelter of the stacked lumber, hopelessly, fearfully waiting. Behind her Mazatlán darkened and slept, the portholes blinked shut, and she paid no attention. She regretted even the brief flare of the match when she lit a cigarette, for that would blind her momentarily to the black harbor mouth. She smoked, untasting, and every ship's lights she saw brought her to the edge of the wharf, pleading that it be the Rainbow returning. Her prayers went unanswered.

During her vigil, she saw the scattered lamps of the Indian freighter, recognizable from its size, pass regally by the bay channel as it turned out onto the Pacific. The sight heightened her loneliness. The freighter had been an integral part of the view from her hotel balcony, but now that view had changed forever, as had everything in her life.

Stiff and shivering occasionally, Cay was still huddled there like a forgotten sentinel as the harbor waters grayed with approaching dawn. Some of the fishing boats were casting loose, stevedores were slumping to work. The renewing light, the first rumbles of awakening commerce promised her that bright daytime would seem even emptier than the night. She had waited in vain. She gazed dully at the empty berth left by the Rainbow. Eventually another boat would dock there. Eventually a derrick would come to hoist away the lumber she sat on. What would she do then? Where should she go?

A curtained black Cadillac made the buttonhook turn off Calzada Miguel Alemán onto the concrete embankment. It crept toward her through the grayness. The headlights played across her and the car stopped, its door slammed softly. Face drawn, Cay rose slowly to her feet, making no attempt to open her purse. Whatever happened, she was past caring.

The slight figure striding forward in the headlamp glow was Diki's. She couldn't make out his face against the light but she could see his scarf, and that he was holding out some small object in his hand.

She heard his voice for the first time; it slurred gently. "You will come along," he said. "He wants to talk to you." There was faint emphasis on "he," the respect due the Trader.

Cay took the object from his hand. It was a small carved teak box, like a jewel case. Her gloved fingers suddenly clumsy, she lifted its hinged lid.

She had been right; it was a jewel case. But no precious gems lay on the white grosgrained silk. All the box contained was a man's little finger, neatly severed. The finger wore a cameo ring, a white classic profile of a Grecian girl's head silhouetted against black, set in gold.

Cay closed the box carefully. She meant to speak but her effort to shape her trembling lips for words drained the last of her strength and she fell fainting into Diki's arms.

Chapter Twenty-Five

Monday, December 10, 6:00 A.M.

Head swimming, she recognized through her veil of despair that she lay huddled in the rear seat of the hearse-like Cadillac as it purred up Cerro del Vigía. Her gloved hands were clenched so tightly that they ached, one holding to her bulky purse, the other clasped about the teak box that contained Walt Kilmer's finger.

The car stopped halfway up the hill. Diki opened the door and she roused herself and got out. He guided her through a broken fence, along a weed-grown path to the doorless portal of a tall mansion where no one could live. For this was Casa Echeguren, the great Tudor house she had noticed often on her jaunts. She knew its story from various drivers, how years before a lover had built it for his fiancée in Spain, a replica of a European chateau she admired; how the girl had died while crossing the ocean to marry him; how, upon its sale, the tragic house had been struck by lightning and burned with the crackling agonies of a bursting heart. Love's ruin, its gutted shell stood in cursed and commanding grandeur on the hillside, charred windows gazing hollow-eyed over city and harbor, peaked walls pointing upward at the heavens that had despoiled it. And the Trader had chosen this desolation for his meeting with Cay Morgan.

She stepped through the doorway alone; Diki waited outside. She moved unsteadily across a waste of old ashes melting into the earth. The interior of the hollow floorless mansion was shadowed ruddily by the dawning of the sun. Above the building's open ramparts—the roof had burned away completely—the sky remained a streaked pall of gray.

She thought momentarily that she waited alone. But a voice spoke her name. She looked up. Short lengths of timber had been studded into the smoky brick walls, forming a crude ladder up to a window of what had been the second story. In that window sat a man, gazing down on her. He commenced to descend the bleak wall, like a pale spider in his white suit, and the binoculars strapped about his neck bobbed against his long thin body.

At last he stood before her. But for the expensive binoculars and his new identity—the Trader—he looked much as she had always seen him. His role had changed but he had not. Nor had his courtly manner, or his appreciative stiff-mustached smile, or his gray mane of hair, or the manicure of his long tanned hands.

"One often overlooks the obvious," said Leonard Trefethen. "For instance, this poor dead house is in plain view of your hotel balcony—a view that works equally well in reverse. Lookout Hill. It's been a very handy lookout for me, both of your comings and goings along Olas Altas and of those of certain boats in which I've had an interest."

Cay swayed slightly. He reached out a hand to steady her but she remained upright. Controlling her voice, she asked faintly, "Is he still alive? You must still have him alive." She tried to find the truth deep in Trefethen's illusive eyes.

With cruel circumspection, he said, "But I ordered you here to tell you what *you* are going to do."

"Tell me about him. Please."

"You're a magnificent woman, Cay, even now. Think how many anxious moments you've caused me in the past week or so. That's all ended, of course. It's been a long night but a successful one." He sighed happily. "If the success weren't so overwhelming—and you so lovely—I might be inclined to bear a grudge. Perhaps you noticed the India freighter that sailed last midnight, precisely on schedule, the ninth of December. It carries a party of Chinese agents—I was dangerously frank with you yesterday evening, my dear—and those gentlemen bear good tidings to Peking. Yes, Spencer Swan has agreed to deal with me."

"I've misjudged the Swans, but I don't care about them."

"Spencer needed a bit of persuasion before he

became willing to sell his hoard to me; he has the Yankee tendency to shop about for bargains. On the other hand, Concha…" Trefethen smiled sensually. "Darling lusty Concha favored my—proposition."

She knew now why Swan had been willing to take her to the island at all; he had wanted her to bid against the Trader. "Do you have Walt at the island now? For God's sake, tell me!" she whispered.

His oblique answer rang in her ears. "In a manner of speaking." Words of torture, revealing nothing. "Your presence that night on the island rendered things awkward for me, Cay, though I do dislike telling you this. Naturally, I knew you were in Mazatlán to try to upset my plans, and I guessed exactly who you were, despite our separation for five years. Your inquiries about Valdes in Tijuana did not go unnoticed, and Diki undertook to head you off. Your marking Diki's forehead supplied the clue. Yet you remained a mere nuisance—until you reached the island."

"That made me worth being killed," she said thinly. "Your needle in my leg, a splash in the ocean. How have you disposed of Walt?"

"Your difficulty is single-mindedness. Notice how my own mind can work on two levels, dear girl. Killing you under those circumstances served a dual purpose: It rid me of you and made the Swans my accomplices, no matter how unwilling, thus binding them more closely with my plans. It takes years of artistry to extemporize like that. I love a dual purpose, don't you? To upset nature with a grand deceit?" Trefethen chuckled.

A dry stricture closed her throat. She stared at him,

his casual gloss, the surface of a human being but with nothing natural inside. She had never been quite able to believe in him, and perhaps he was as entirely hollow as this eerie gutted house he used. She could understand now her inability to find him for so long. The Trader *was* a phantom; he didn't actually exist except during the play of his own deceits. A puffball, a layered surface of composite lie, nothing tangible.

"Unfortunately," he said, "your life seems to be as charmed as my own. Thanks that night to the unknown presence of your Mr. Kilmer and his little boat."

He had mentioned Walt on purpose, goading her. Her hand tightened about the little box. She managed to ask again, "Where is he now?"

Trefethen put a finger to his chin, seeming to muse. "Ordinarily I am opposed to indiscriminate killing. I can usually conceive a better rebuke—as your forehead will attest."

Her well of bitterness overflowed. "Did you tell George Hodd that? Did you tell Walt that?"

"Ordinarily, I said." He shrugged. "On the brink of such a fortune as this... after all, what are one or two indefinite lives compared to the absolute truth of gold?"

"Our lives are not indefinite, damn you! You're the freak, you're the monster!"

"Oh, we're all God's little beasties and I love my fellow creatures as well as you do, I'm sure." The sun had risen higher; an errant beam gave Trefethen's face a sheen as if it were molded of wax. "You were breaking into *my* life, Cay—first things first. I had to take steps to protect the all-important self. With Hodd, gullible chap, it was easily done. But you complicated matters by joining forces not only with Kilmer, who is a representative of the law, but with D'Hureau."

"*Is?*" cried Cay, seizing upon the tense he used. "Walt is alive?"

Again Trefethen's answer slid aside. "The problem of surveillance was a neat one. But worthwhile, since eventually you led me to D'Hureau, who'd been impossible to locate heretofore. There was your seductive contretemps with Swan, of course, but my luck saved me there just as yours saved you from Diki's talented hands in the public market." He paused ruefully. "In fact, dear Cay, Dame Fortune smiles on you oftener than you perhaps know. You should be dead three times over. I fully expected that D'Hureau's wine—"

"I was delayed," she murmured listlessly. "D'Hureau—Felix—they weren't." She heard Trefethen laugh.

"Well!" he said. "I didn't realize the bottle trap would encompass Señor Felix also. How much tidier that way! Not that the foolish Mexican mattered. D'Hureau was the focal point, the filthy pig. He was a traitor, you know, the murderer of my old friend Valdes. I regret nothing about D'Hureau except that I missed seeing his last drinking bout. I do confess I viewed your own escape last night with mixed emotions. Odd that I should feel so attracted to any opponent, Cay."

She shuddered at his caressing words. She didn't

feel that she could stand on her feet much longer. "But Walt—please—what have you—"

"Yes, your lover. I tried to separate you two yesterday evening by revealing Kilmer's true status to you. I believed your emotional involvement with him might destroy any more interference on both your parts. Sadly enough, Kilmer hadn't waited for you. He took last night in his own hands. A foolish crusade, as it's turned out. Yes, he's clever, ferocious even—but foolish."

Cay trembled. Trefethen was hovering over the one fact she wanted to know. In the roofless lightening sky above flapped the inquisitive black wings of a carrion bird.

Trefethen smiled blandly at her. "See how tightly you hold in your hand that little gem box that brought you here? Well, your Walt Kilmer is now just as tightly in my hands."

Her pent-up breath sobbed out of her. *Walt was alive!* The gaunt looming walls of the ruined house whirled about her. "Thank God," she whispered. "Thank God!"

Trefethen's solicitous hand was cupped under her elbow, his warm breath touching her cheek as he kept her from collapsing. "Thank me," he corrected her. She shook free of him. He laughed again. "One of my failings is admiration of a stout fight, even in my enemies. It's easier with thoroughly whipped enemies, I'll admit. Now that you can understand your position in relation to mine, perhaps I'll allow you to strike a bargain."

"I only want him back," she said feebly. "Anything."

"You want him back. Precisely. For myself, I only want to be left in peace. It'll take a certain amount of time to dig up the gold I've bought and get it ready for shipment aboard the India freighter when it returns. May I be allowed to do that without interference, my dear? Of course, I can have you finished off, and Kilmer as well, but every man to his own methods. Do you want to hear my conditions?"

She nodded dumbly.

"First, the lump of gold that I know you stole from D'Hureau's house. I insist on its return to me, merely as a point of honor. Second, you will leave Mazatlán immediately and forever. I've chosen your place of exile, a small Mexican village named San Felipe, at the head of the Gulf, sufficiently out of my way." He eyed her closely. "You appear tractable so far, eh? I've arranged for your transportation. This morning at nine you will board a private plane at the airport for the journey. Diki will keep you company during the trip. Simply to make certain you don't exert your considerable charm on the pilot."

"But Walt—"

"Kilmer will remain in my possession until my transactions here are completed. After that, I will forward him to you in San Felipe. From then on, you two may consider yourselves free to romp about wherever you choose. I'm positive our paths will never cross again. Do you know why? Because the next time would be frightful for both of you."

"You'll send him to me? You won't…" She couldn't say the words.

"Oh, yes, I'll forward Kilmer to you *alive*. Alive and

unharmed—except for that one small finger, which you can consider as a deposit. I don't demand even an entire pound of flesh, do I?" He chuckled, a metallic sound as of the closing of a trap. "What long ago began as insurance has become a conceit of mine. The Trader must always mark his former opposition in some way."

Cay opened her purse and removed the lump of gold. As she handed it over, her dark-gloved fingers turned rigid with frustration. What Trefethen didn't know was that her purse also contained D'Hureau's automatic pistol; Trefethen still believed he had kept guns beyond her reach. Yet the possession of the weapon availed her nothing. For five years she had sought this moment, to face the Trader with the means to kill him. And here was her climax. With one quick movement, her finger squeezing in luxurious bitterness around the trigger, she could fire through the purse and the Trader would thrash about dying on the ashy ground. All she had ever wanted...

Except that she wanted Walt more. He had made her wholly a woman. Walt was her climax now; love was her climax, not hate. Because of him, she made her sacrifice. She closed the purse and asked quietly, "What guarantee do I have that you'll do as you say?"

"None at all," he said in his brittle voice. "You may only hope." Lifting her cold hand gallantly, Trefethen pressed his lips to the back of its doeskin glove. "And now, Cay dear, let me wish you *bon voyage*."

Chapter Twenty-Six

Wednesday, January 16, 10:00 A.M.

Cay slashed another date off the calendar. That made the thirty-eighth X mark, over a month since the beginning of her exile. She sneezed and then swore dismally at the way sneezing aroused her headache. She had drunk too much last night, she had been drinking too much every night to kill the dragging loneliness and the worry and the heavy boredom. And so this morning her head was splitting and her stomach churned.

She trudged to the window and looked out at the sunny day. Night had wrought no miracles; nothing had changed in the flat adobe surroundings. She moaned, feeling old. And when, turning, she saw her lackluster eyes in the bureau mirror, she shuddered. Her shoulders drooped. She reached for her brandy, stopped her hand in time, and flung herself across the bed, sobbing.

These were her depths of despair. She had been humbled, broken; her fires had gone out and she feared she would never be her ardently alive self again. Even in those high moments when she made herself believe in Walt's eventual release, she doubted if he could love the whipped Cay Morgan as intensely as her former self.

The Trader had chosen a barren exile for her. San

Felipe was a primitive fishing village on the rugged gulf coast of Baja California, 125 miles south of the border. A shabby wilderness town, it had built up a few tourist accommodations since the black-top highway had pushed down from Mexicali, and Cay got a room in a low rambling white adobe hotel south of town.

Having no interest in fishing, she had quickly exhausted all that the town and its sand dunes had to offer. For hours she had watched the swarthy villagers mend nets and repair boats on the wide yellow beach. She had tired of overhearing American dialogues about forty-eight-pound test lines, wire leaders, four-ounce weights, the bait value of dead sardines against jigs or plugs. She had eaten in all the cafés, drunk in all the cantinas, visited the shell-necklace factory, and watched the village barber shave customers by flash-light. With the advent of Christmas, even the tourists had vanished homeward. She had been left alone with her fear.

She forced herself to rise from the bed. She dressed in her sleeveless black linen and sandals, and escaped from her room and the empty brandy bottles lining the bureau. Here, the sunny air was more dryly crisp than in Mazatlán, but its ripe fragrance—fish and poverty mingled—didn't help her stomach any. Wistfully she looked up the dark ribbon of highway where her fellow Americans had disappeared in their gleaming new cars. As far as she could see, the road was bare. So was the hollow blue sky. San Felipe's landing strip wasn't on any airline's regular schedule.

She walked by habit into the town, a gritty cluster of adobe walls around an arid plaza. The weathered

buildings, strung together with fences of gulf drift-
wood, housed five hundred souls altogether, but
seldom exhibited more than a few urchins playing in
the dusty streets, some loungers in front of a cantina,
or a mangy dog.

Thirty minutes of slow walking took her from one
end of town to the other and along the golden stretch
of beach—a half mile wide now that the gigantic gulf
tide was out—and finally to her daily visit to the sport-
fishing office. The Mexican dreaming behind the desk
had seen her every morning during the past month.
He droned the usual answers. No, there was no com-
munication from Mazatlán on any subject whatsoever.
No, there were no ships expected to anchor in the tiny
inlet. Planes? "*Quién sabe, Señora?* They come
without warning."

Her face felt taut and flushed. She wondered about
recurrent tropic fever; her mild attacks had ceased
years ago and she had given up carrying quinine. But,
as much for diversion as relief, she wandered across
the plaza to the office of Dr. Ignacio Peña. San
Felipe's only physician, as time-laden as she, was
delighted to have a patient. He insisted upon a complete physical examination. The fever existed only in
her imagination and he denied her quinine. Dr. Peña's
prescription, when stripped of his florid exhortations,
was for less liquor, more sleep, and general freedom
from troubles of the mind. He did give her a few
aspirins.

Cay sat on the yellow beach sands and thought
about it, while she twisted Walt Kilmer's cameo ring
around and around on her knuckle. She wore it as a

wedding ring on her left hand, drawing what comfort she could from that tiny bond with him. The rest of the Trader's gift to her—the teak jewel box and its human content—she had consecrated to the sea during her first day here. Oh, Walt, she prayed silently to the sparkling blue water, please come soon, because I need you so much.

A faint distant humming made her squint up against the hot sky, and she saw the answer to her prayer. Breathless, she watched the winged speck enlarge into the silvery shape of a twin-engine transport. It roared overhead and her hope died. Then the craft banked gracefully to return. Its wheels began to lower...

Cay sprang up excitedly. Heedless of her throbbing head and stomach, she trotted down the beach toward the landing strip a half mile away. Then, seeing that she would arrive nearly as soon as the airplane, she slowed to a fast walk, holding the ship constantly with her eyes so that it wouldn't vanish magically. The station wagon that the sport-fishing office operated as a sometime taxi passed by her, its balloon tires spurting sand.

The plane thundered over her head and bounced down onto the dirt runway. It made its far-end turn and came trundling back toward the air-sock tower. Cay reached the tower itself as the engine roar died. The ship's side door opened and unfolded its stairway. Passengers emerged, stretching and blinking.

She couldn't breathe for watching them. One by one they descended, but none approximated Walt's burly body, his sunburned blunt face. Cay's hopes shriveled. The last couple was an international mixture, the man Mexican, the woman American. Like the others, they headed for the station wagon. Cay turned away, her strained eyes hot with disappointment.

And then she whirled back quickly, every nerve alert. The mixed couple had *not* been the last passengers. Another man, dark-suited, appeared hastily upon the flimsy gangway. He paused to slick back his hair and adjust his dark glasses, then trailed after the others.

Cay stepped back against the air-sock tower and waited. As the man came by she reached for his arm, hesitantly, as if expecting her hand to pass through a phantom body.

"I thought you were dead," she told him.

A start of surprise, then the man achieved a debonair grin. "As you can see, *huera*, that is a gross lie," said Rómulo María Felix.

Chapter Twenty-Seven

Wednesday, January 16, 1:00 P.M.

Of all the fantastic notions blurring through her mind, Cay fastened on the only one vital to her. "You've brought a message for me!" she declared. "That's why you've come!"

Felix removed his dark glasses and goggled at her, his full lips curling scornfully. "Believe this—had I known *you* were here, my mistress of trouble, I should never have come. Never!"

Her faith was crushed again. "Then why—"

His eyes slid warily toward the last couple off the plane. They were climbing into the station wagon with the others. "The call of business. Profitable, I presume, since that well-to-do pair, both married to still other fools, have come here to adulterate. We've traveled all the way from Ciudad Mexico together, we three, although my companions are unaware of my function. I see they are escaping me. I must…"

Cay tucked her arm under his. "Don't tug so," she murmured. "Smile cheerfully at me or I'll spill your beans to those people. I should do it anyway, just on principle."

"*Caray!*" groaned Felix. "Time hasn't dulled your claws at all."

He did work up a smile as they joined the load in the station wagon. Most of the passengers were taken to the sport-fishing office. The couple Felix was tailing—they looked deeply in love, Cay thought enviously—had reservations at the hotel at which Cay was staying. Riding together, they all exchanged banal pleasantries while Cay pondered the insecurities and cruel whimsies of life. How could one ever pierce the human exterior to see the true motives? For example, the unaware couple from Mexico City who chatted gaily with Felix—how could they know that his presence here was motivated by their passion?

Felix had similar thoughts but he approached them from a characteristic self-adulatory angle. "How amusing it is," he confided to Cay as they sat in the cantina of the hotel, keeping surreptitious tabs on his quarry in another booth. "They consider themselves free as birds. Yet all the time Rómulo María Felix hovers over them like the angel of destruction."

"Speaking of destruction," Cay prompted, "I'm slightly curious as to how you returned from the dead."

"Ah, *huera*, I was never dead."

"Not really!"

"Truly. I don't know by how many minutes I escaped the fates. When I attended our appointment immediately after sundown, poor D'Hureau had already succumbed to the effects of the poisoned wine. Cyanide, *verdad?* A horrible sight. My shocked brain hadn't yet recovered when I heard your taxi arrive out front."

"But why the act?"

Felix dropped his glance sheepishly. "Forgive me, but the idea came over me that perhaps it was *you* who planned to murder your associates, and that you were returning to observe the results. Being cornered anyway, I feigned death to test my theory."

"But surely you could tell how surprised I was."

"Could I? Again forgive me, but your actions—robbing D'Hureau of both his gold and his pistol—did nothing to reassure me. I nearly swooned, fearing you might examine my corpse. From that moment on, I knew that the Mazatlán affair was not my dish." He nodded toward the couple he had followed to San Felipe. "This is a far pleasanter practicing of the detective profession."

"Don't you mean the blackmail profession?"

Felix shrugged, grinned, and motioned to the bartender to refill their glasses. A plate of tacos and withered salad sat on the booth table before them, the food required by the drinking laws. After a casual sip of his bourbon, Felix inquired, "Whatever did happen to D'Hureau's golden nugget? Simple curiosity."

Cay told him. Felix listened, mouth open, while she told of her final hours in Mazatlán, the revelation of Walt Kilmer's official status, the long night watch at the harborside, and finally the dawn encounter with Trefethen, the Trader, within the smoky walls of Casa Echeguren.

"Espíritu santo!" breathed Felix when she'd finished. "My instincts were right, as usual, when they directed me to forsake Mazatlán that night. And you— you are lucky to be here alive."

"Am I? How lucky? To be completely alone in this void, without him— Oh, I don't suppose you can see what it's doing to me."

"Well, perhaps a certain sallowness in the cheeks…"

Cay chuckled edgily. "That comes from a steady diet of one's own heart, morning, noon, and night. Actually, the doctor says I'm healthy as an ox. His exact words." She grimaced. "I've never sat still so long in my life. 'You must lose your woes,' said the doctor. Well, I could fish for eight different kinds of fish here, but I can't stand fish. Movies every other night, but I detest a smelly theatre. Oh, yes, on Saturday nights there's a big public dance next to El Puerto Café. Oh, damn, I don't mean to cry."

"And all for the sake of love," sighed Felix admiringly. "You've so much more heart than I imagined, *huera.*" He rose and went to the bar, where a spray of red roses bloomed in a vase. Disregarding the bartender's glare, he broke off the largest blossom and brought it back to Cay. Felix presented it solemnly, "For your sufferings, señora."

She smiled embarrassedly. "Thank you, my friend. However, despite my outburst, it might be far worse. There could be no hope at all."

"True. I was fortunate to escape such a marooning as you've had. In fact, I recall that I've been doubly fortunate. Only a few days ago, in Ciudad Mexico, I espied Señor Trefethen on a path in Alameda Park. I very nearly spoke to him." Felix shuddered. "What a narrow one! He might have murdered me on sight. He might have— What affects you?"

Cay stared at the red rose in her hands. A numbing rigidity seemed to creep over her limbs, into her heart and her brain, as if she were turning to stone.

"I believe you are really not well," cried Felix.

She shook her head dazedly and dropped the rose to the floor. "I'm all right," she mumbled as she stood up. "Wait for me. I'll come back…"

She found herself holding to the hotel registration desk and inquiring of the clerk's curious eyes, "May I use the telephone? I wish to call El Centro, California." And then the instrument was perspiring in her grasp and she talked to operator after operator until finally a faraway bell rang.

A man answered with a gruff monosyllable. Cay said, "Hello. I must speak to Rexie Boston."

The man made her repeat it, then said, "Sorry. Don't know anybody by that name around here."

"This is Cay Morgan. Catherine Morgan. I have to locate him."

"That you, Cay?" the distant voice shouted. "Why the hell didn't you say so first? With the roust being on the border, I got to take care who I talk to these days."

"Rexie, I need help fast. Is your plane in shape?"

"The day it isn't, I'll go broke."

"I'm in San Felipe. I want a lift tonight, going south. Just a ride, nothing else, no contraband."

"There's a nasty word," Rexie Boston warned, laughing. "You know I'd break my neck for you, Cay beautiful. How soon you expect me?"

They settled the time and details, then Cay returned to Felix. He looked up at the inflexible lines of her face apprehensively. "Felix, how'd you like to go back to Mazatlán with me tonight?"

"No, *huera,* I think I'd prefer not."

"You will, nevertheless. I may need help settling the score. A plane will pick us up tonight at eight."

She left him abruptly and went to her room. She packed her belongings, the incense burner, the Madeira lace runner, the gilt-framed silhouettes of her "parents," all her fine clothes. She dressed herself for action, pulling the dark blue slacks over her legs, donning the pull-over sweater and jacket that matched. The black silk bandanna again hid her pearl-blonde hair, the wide-cuffed doeskin gloves were stuck in her belt, the low soft boots shod her feet.

Having clothed herself, she wrote a short letter and posted it in the box labeled *"Buzón"* in the lobby. And lastly, she cleaned and oiled the Lahti pistol that had belonged to D'Hureau.

Cay Morgan was returning to Mazatlán because there was no longer any reason to continue her exile.

She knew at last that her lover was dead.

Chapter Twenty-Eight

Thursday, January 17, 1:00 A.M.

Rexie Boston put his plane over in a steep bank so Cay could look down through the side window. "That the place?" he shouted above the engine roar.

Cay stared at the tiny blob far below them, the pale-rimmed black opal of land set against the glassy murk of the sea. In the distance, a faint scatter of lights showed the location of Mazatlán. She patted Boston's shoulder with a gloved hand and nodded. They were over the Isla de Puesta del Sol.

It had been a long cool trip, nearly five hours in the twin-engined Beechcraft, hurtling without lights through the moonless night. The sturdy dark-painted ship was not built for comfort, all rear seats having been removed to increase the cargo capacity. So she and Felix had sat or crouched on the metal floor, unable to pass time even in conversation because of the thunder of power holding them aloft.

Not that Cay felt like talking. Her hand moved often to the cumbersome pistol thrust in her waistband.

On the black spot of island below, a light flickered, was momentarily lost, flickered again. Cay pressed her

forehead against the window, studying the phe-
nomenon grimly. From its southerly location, the light
didn't come from Swan's plantation house. "The
Trader," she whispered, knowing her deductions had
proved correct but feeling little satisfaction in the
proof. The Trader was on the island, laboring at night
to unearth the gold ingots. Furthermore, since he
believed he had overcome all dangerous interference,
Cay doubted that he would allow any of the island's
native guards to be posted within discovery distance of
the treasure cache. Indeed, why should he believe in
the need for guards at all at this stage of the game? His
greatest security lay in isolation.

"Hold tight," Boston hollered. "We're riding down
for a look-see." He heeled his plane over into a
whistling dive. He had a young but battered face with
pouchy eyes and silky handlebar mustaches. The
leather jacket straining across his shoulders bore
mended flak holes from Berlin.

Ears popping, they hurtled down into warmer,
moister air and circled Sunset Island from a distance
offshore, a distance sufficient for the pounding of the
surf to cover their engine hum. Cay couldn't see the
flicker of light now. She watched Boston instead as his
keen eyes reconnoitered the beaches. Finally he held
up a hand, making an O of thumb and forefinger. "If
the sand's as hard as you say," he yelled, "that beach
there on the ocean side is our ticket." He grinned at
his passengers. "Unless we trip over a dune or something."

Felix groaned.

Boston headed his ship out to sea, gradually losing

altitude as he swung parallel to the mysterious shore, at last banking a final approach toward the long silvery beach. He cut the engines and aimed the plane's stubby nose at the straight strip of sand. The only sound in the cabin was the buzz of air streaming by them. The sand heaved up to meet them, raced beneath the windows. The wheels touched smoothly, with scarcely a jar, and they slowed as Boston applied the brakes.

Felix was praising every saint in the calendar. Cay experienced nothing; she had been certain they would reach the island safely, with a certainty that had nothing to do with Boston's ability as a pilot. She knew her own ruthless destiny would deliver her here for the final showdown. Hands more skeletal than Boston's were at the wheel tonight.

"Well, Cay beautiful, we're here," said Boston as the Beechcraft rolled to a quiet stop. "What's next on our list?"

She unlocked the door. "I'll play it from now on. Are you satisfied that you can take off from here too, Rexie?"

"I never land where I can't get out of."

"Then wait for me. When you see me returning, start the engines."

Felix cleared his throat. "Forgive me, *huera*, but I don't advise you to attempt this venture alone." He waved at the rows of tall nodding palms that edged the beach like drowsy ogres.

"Don't tell me you want to come along."

"I most absolutely do not," said Felix shakily. "I find this whole enterprise as rewarding as a nightmare.

Nevertheless"—a nervous shrug—"I am your friend. I shall accompany you."

Cay patted his knee gently. "Thanks, my friend. I'll remember that always. It's reassuring to know you're here if I need you, but I must do this alone, if I can." Her glance challenged Boston. "Any objections from you, Rexie?"

"It's your show." He fingered the automatic in her small fist. "But I got a suggestion." He reached up to the roof of the cabin and pressed a catch. A hinged section fell away and he disengaged a short carbine from the rack there. He slapped a fifteen-round magazine into place and offered the gun to Cay. "Care to increase your fire power, beautiful?"

She seized the .30-caliber rifle gratefully and handed him the clumsy pistol. "If I'm not back in an hour, the two of you might come looking."

"Don't worry," said Boston. "I know the voice of my carbine. Any other artillery speaks up, we'll be there, but fast."

She waved back at them from the first fringe of palm trees and then plunged into the darkness of the grove, bearing toward the location of the light she had spotted from the air. Despite the thick gloom of the humid night, progress at first was easy and rapid. No underbrush had been allowed to grow between the even rows of palm trunks. As her watchful eyes adjusted to the lack of illumination, she strode along without stumbling, almost as if she were on a city street. The spiked fronds whispered raspingly high over her head.

Then the palms decreased in size, newer plantings,

as she neared the edge of the vast grove. Where the slim trees halted altogether, the native vegetation rose abruptly as a tangled barrier. She could sight no opening and so forced her way directly into this uncultivated portion of Swan's island. Her rifle butt gouged a passage, and dank ferns swept across her face and serpentine vines twined with seeming purpose about her trousered legs. Step by step she wormed her way through the resilient web of greenery, her clothes dripping with perspiration and juice from torn plants, until she came upon the trail she had known must exist. The trail was not cut, only trampled, a narrow one-person aisle overhung with oozing branches. She reversed her rifle, barrel first, and crept along cautiously.

Presently she stopped motionless, her ears tuned to an alien sound among the chirping jungle noises. The sound continued, only a short distance away, and she identified it at last as the creak of a windlass. She eased forward noiselessly, crouching as she moved toward a glimmer through the foliage. The glimmer grew steadily in brilliance as she approached. And she looked finally on what she had come to see.

A room-size square of the snarled vegetation had been chopped away, the damp earth scraped clear. Within these verdant walls, a pit had been dug in the jungle floor. Kerosene lanterns on stakes, screened except from above, lighted the pit's mouth yellowly. The dancing rays glowed over a tarpaulin-shrouded heap at one side of the clearing. Where the canvas flapped loose at a corner of the pile, Cay could see the neatly stacked ends of age-blackened ingots. The lamplight glanced dully off the metal of the long-barreled pistol that lay on top of the covered treasure heap; the yellow rays glistened on the sweaty muscles of the lone man laboring over the small windlass.

Cay stood erect and stepped out of the shadows and leveled the carbine at the Trader's spine.

"Turn around," she commanded in a clear voice. "I shouldn't care to shoot you in the back, Walt."

Chapter Twenty-Nine

Thursday, January 17, 2:00 A.M.

He spun around. The winch cable, freed of his restraining grasp, whipped downward to clank its burden on the unseen bottom of the pit. Across the dark gaping hole he had dug, they faced each other. Stripped to the waist, muscles bulged taut with surprise, his cropped black curls damp with exertion, Walt Kilmer looked much as she had first seen him aboard the Rainbow. But appearance meant little; a greater gulf than the pit yawned between them now.

She stood in silence, waiting for him to speak. She watched comprehension grow in his gray eyes as he looked at the carbine pointed at his belly. Knowing him so well at last, Cay could follow every question in his mind. Should he try for his pistol on top of the ingot heap three long strides away? Or should he use other weapons, await better chances? She watched him decide on the latter course. He raised his eyes to hers. "Well, Cay. It must have been very dull at San Felipe."

"I had time to think." Her voice was normal.

"You should have waited there."

"You'd never have come."

"No. How could I? But San Felipe was best for you."

Even the timbre of his voice had changed. She could no longer identify it as American; his English might have been learned anywhere. His stance, his weather-beaten features had undergone subtle alteration. For he was no longer playing the ingenuous tramp fisherman; he had returned to the devious complexities of his own true identity—which, as the Trader, amounted to almost no identity at all.

Cay's lip curled. "We'll abandon all the make-believe, won't we, Walt? I know we're alone here. You wouldn't allow anybody within a mile of this place, not with the gold lying around."

"You're right—secrecy ensures trust. I can be frank with you. The Swans are asleep at their house, both Diki and Trefethen are off in Ciudad Mexico, and as for the plantation workers—well, we are very alone together, Cay. As we were on one other night."

"Yes. I'm considering how I had you at my mercy, all that night. But I didn't know, Walt; that's my excuse. Why didn't you kill me?"

His cynical mouth grinned. "You've always come up with the oddest angles. Why should I kill you unnecessarily? We were enjoying ourselves, you can't fool me about that."

"I don't intend to."

"Kill you, Cay? I look on death as generally super-
fluous and often hazardous. I prefer to mark my enemies for future reference. That's usually proved good
enough to ensure no future reference necessary." He
chuckled abruptly and shook his head at her tenderly.
"This'll come as a blow to your vanity, sweetheart, but
damned if I remembered who you were until I had
you unconscious on the Rainbow. Until I accidentally
uncovered the scar on your forehead. Five years is a
long busy time."

He could have said nothing to shock her more. Five
years of her life had been dedicated to wiping out an
injury that he hadn't even remembered! "I'm flat-
tered," she said, and her voice trembled against her
will. But the carbine remained steady in her gloved
hands. "I must have been good company to be still
alive tonight. You won everything I had, everything I
knew, my entire fool's confidence, even my gratitude.
You had the cards stacked when you began working on
me with that trick rescue." She bared her teeth
fiercely. "You made a splendid hero. I wonder why I
never remembered how big the ocean is. I didn't have
one chance in a billion of being fished out of the sea
the way you told it."

"Vanity again," Walt assured her, and shrugged.
"We never believe the odds apply to our own selves.
But you're right. Trefethen drugged you and brought
you to the Rainbow. I dunked you a time or two and
the stage was set."

"With all the props. Gratitude. Confidence. And…"

"Love," he finished curtly. "Why make such an epic
out of it? So we had a battle royal and I won it. We

both enjoyed the battle, at bedtime anyway, so we're even there."

"Should I hate you any less for being right?"

"Like all women, your emotions are out of balance." The lantern light wavered over his half-naked body, making him a figure in a tropical dream. "But you were a splendid animal when you pushed your emotions to the limits, far better when you were acting on them than when you were acting on your reason. Yet I had to keep close watch on you. Some of your stabs in the dark almost made me forget you were nothing but a damned woman."

"I've learned that," she said. "I am a damned woman."

"Sorry for yourself? Don't be, Cay. For example, your twilight tête-à-tête with Spencer Swan. My interrupting that wasn't accidental, you know. I'll admit it backfired on me—but no worse than it did on you. Diki had been instructed to keep Swan from falling into your hands at all costs. If I hadn't arrived at the public market in time to flag him off your neck..."

"Then you'd have spent a lonely Saturday night."

He grinned at her, the same fond grin of the lover she had once given herself to. "You don't regret that night. You mustn't."

Not regret trickery... not regret her greatest gift insidiously turned against herself, her pure ecstasy secretly alloyed and molded into weapons of deceit? She said thickly, "You staged everything to find out what I knew, and what D'Hureau knew. You wanted me to lead you to D'Hureau. Once I'd done that, you didn't need me alive any longer."

"I had another mistress, remember—expediency." He sighed, his sinewy features twisting ruefully. "The ninth of December was a complicated day, even for me. The Chinese agents were due to sail, Swan was being stubborn about the gold transaction, and then you insisted on carrying out that crazy invasion scheme at once. What choice did I have? I had to force Swan to give guarantees to the Peking buyers, and at the same time halt you and D'Hureau without giving myself away. I am glad you escaped the poison. I hadn't counted on Concha's attack on you, but I was glad it turned out that way."

Cay laughed shortly. "Poor Concha. I thought she threw the acid at my face because she was jealous of my playing around with her husband. Concha was jealous, all right, but I picked the wrong man. She was jealous of her lover—you. She had seen you with me Saturday night. Poor Concha! You scarcely had time for the two of us at once, did you?"

"Swan insisted on shopping about for a better price on the gold," said Walt. "Yes, Concha served as a great lever of influence for my terms—though I finally had to use different, quicker levers to bring Swan around to my point of view."

There was a brief silence, only the wilderness stirring softly. Then Cay murmured, "I've been wondering whose finger was in the box you sent me. So it was Swan's. Extremely clever, Walt, and extremely heartless." She hoisted the rifle and snapped, "No closer to that pistol!"

Walt ceased his slow crablike edging and said affectionately, "I'm only interested in talking sense to you,

Cay. We can't do it under these circumstances."

"Oh, spare me the loving-kindness!" she cried. "That doesn't fit you any better than that cock-and-bull story about the federal agent."

"Trefethen is a cock-and-bull expert, occasionally grandiose but a brilliant liar. When he saw that you had escaped D'Hureau's wine, he improvised that story on the spur of the moment. Simply to keep you from discovering I had sailed from Mazatlán to wind up my own business. Well, you discovered my absence anyway, but Trefethen had spun so well that you completely misinterpreted my actions. So we played it your way and exiled you to San Felipe. A case where love served as well as death."

"And afterwards? What did you expect I'd do when I'd eaten my heart out and you still hadn't come?"

He shrugged. "You'd have supposed I was dead. You'd have returned to Mazatlán to discover nothing. My identity was safe, and I was willing to risk Trefethen's hide should you ever catch up with him again." Walt looked at her tense dark-clad figure across the pit. "Cay," he said comfortingly, and would have moved around the crater to her side, but she thrust the carbine forward with a snarl. He froze and spoke carefully. "Trefethen bragged to me that he did a marvelous job posing as the Trader. Apparently you weren't so taken in as he believed. He sometimes overreaches."

"No. He did well." Cay wondered, staring at his powerful body poised for an animal rush that might come any instant. How had she ever been taken in by Trefethen? No such trivial man could have survived as the Trader so long. The Trader had to be the kind of creature who waited his moment across the pit, the creature his tortuous career had proved he must be—a brute, cunning and jungle-wise. She could read in Walt's eyes a stubborn slyness she had never detected before, and she could reinterpret the moody savagery of his sun-baked face. She whispered, "Walt, you left me too long in San Felipe. I had too much time to think about you. Then today I was handed a rose, a red rose…"

He didn't understand. He watched her narrowly.

"Trefethen sent me roses to the hotel. He was pretending to believe that I'd only been taken ill that night at the Swans'. Now if he'd been the soap representative he pretended to be, he might have done just that. But if he was the Trader, he'd never have done it. The Trader presumably believed me drowned, and he wouldn't have called attention in any way to the fact that he'd been with me that night on the island, since my death would inevitably be investigated. Well, Trefethen turned out to be an enemy, all right, and implicated in my drowning. And yet he *had* sent me the roses. Which meant he'd never really believed me drowned. All that added up to the fact that the drowning had to be a fake—*and the rescue was a fake too!*" She smiled thinly at his expression. "Merely a feminine remembrance of flowers. All female emotion and no reason, eh?"

He argued, "You must have had more to go on than that!"

"Certainly, once I started. All the coincidences and discrepancies that had slipped by me. George Hodd's death, for instance. Only two persons in Mazatlán knew he was connected with me. Felix saw us together on a Monday—but George wasn't killed until the following Thursday, immediately after *you* met him."

"That was a regrettable accident," Walt said. "Hodd was too thorough for his own safety. He came snooping around the Rainbow. Unfortunately, Diki and I were together. So he had to be silenced by falling off the pergola."

"Regrettable accident," echoed Cay. "Well, the regret remains that I should have recognized you sooner. I should have wondered why Trefethen revealed his Trader identity to me so readily when the Trader had been such a secret all these years. I should have wondered when Trefethen sent me away from Mazatlán. Why should Trefethen think that Walt Kilmer meant that much to me? That was *your* ego at work. Only you knew that love was more important to me than revenge."

Walt stood silent, brow furrowed. After a moment, he said, "And now, it's only the gold that matters." He stared deep into her eyes, his mouth quirked, and he gestured at the tarpaulined stack of ingots. "There lies our future, Cay, solid objects that we can talk sense about. I told you how highly I've thought of you before—but never so highly as tonight. There's never been a woman like you."

"Or a man like you," she said quietly.

"What if we started over again, you and I together?" His gaze shone with passionate sincerity. "Look there—we have more money between us then we need in a dozen lifetimes. And that's only half of what's still in the ground. What if we devoted it to one lifetime, ours? Go to a place neither of us has ever been, settle down, perhaps raise a—"

She burst into mocking laughter. "Nobody can spend that gold, Walt, neither you nor any of your scummy crew. Before I left San Felipe I mailed a letter to the Mexican government. I told them all about the ingots. They'll take over the island soon enough, don't worry."

He had flushed to his shoulders at her laugh but he strained to control his voice. "All right. Forget the gold, but for God's sake, remember us. Remember what we've had already. We can be happy."

"Once that was all I wanted," Cay said harshly. "I could have done without gold or revenge, because I'd have had you." She took her left hand away from the carbine and opened her fingers. Lying on the palm of her glove was his cameo ring. When he had seen it, she tilted her hand and let the ring vanish into the pit. It made no sound. "And now I am going to kill you, Walt."

For the first time his rugged features softened in confusion but it was only a brief glimpse of fear. He couldn't see beyond the pale set lines of her face, into her brain, where the fiery cross of vengeance raged hungrily, a headless cross like a T written in flame. So he dared to say soothingly, "Cay, I realize how this last month has put you on edge. Occasionally cruelty can't be helped. Those times are past—the times of being cruel to each other. The hours we spent together were no fake, you know that. We swore it once—I'm your man just as you're my woman. I'm your lover."

"No," said Cay flatly. "My lover is dead."

Walt shook his head. He grinned tenderly. "But, darling, I'm not afraid of you. You know why? Because we're so much alike. You wouldn't harm part of yourself. You couldn't have fallen in love so quickly and so deeply except with one of your own kind, could you? Oh, you're hurt and bitter now, but later on…" He held out his strong arms to her. "Come here and kiss me," he commanded gently.

She squeezed the trigger and watched the bullet make a hole in the hard-muscled expanse of chest she had loved. The wound bloomed as redly as a rosebud, and she watched impassively as the hands that had caressed her came struggling up to cover the mortal injury she had inflicted. She saw agony sponge the incredulity off his face. Walt Kilmer sank to his knees before her, then plunged headlong into the pit.

She leaned over the lip of the hole. Walt lay sprawled on his back, ten feet down, staring upward at her. In the lantern light his lips seemed to move. She pointed the gun barrel again and squeezed back the trigger until at last the rifle was empty. She stood there above the pit, her eyelids closed over a throbbing darkness within her head, while the echoes lost themselves in the silent jungle. Finally she opened her eyes and turned away from the clearing.

She staggered along the path she had come, her face hot with tears but burdened with cold heaviness inside her limbs and body. Branches lashed at her but she felt nothing. She moved faster, stumbling blindly, to escape the loving laugh she imagined pursued her through the darkness, and the voice that said, "I prefer to mark my enemies for future reference…"

Yet she knew that, no matter how fast she ran or how far, Cay Morgan could never escape the bitter natural jest. Even in death, the Trader had marked her again. The doctor in San Felipe had told her so that morning. Within her, growing, growing, in grim retribution, she carried his child.

THE END